STRANGE ISLANDS

PHILIP STANIER

Typeset by inkCONCRETE in Garamond

inkCONCRETE

www.inkconcrete.co.uk

STRANGE ISLANDS

Dedication.

For my Children, Family and Friends.

Seek and learn to recognise who and what, in the midst of the inferno, are not inferno, then make them endure, give them space.

Italo Calvino, Invisible Cities ✗

Be not afeard; the isle is full of noises,
Sounds and sweet airs, that give delight, and hurt not.
Sometimes a thousand twangling instruments
Will hum about mine ears; and sometime voices,
That, if I then had waked after long sleep,
Will make me sleep again: and then, in dreaming,
The clouds methought would open, and show riches
Ready to drop upon me; that, when I waked,
I cried to dream again.

William Shakespeare, The Tempest

Once there were brook trout in the streams in the mountains. You could see them standing in the amber current where the white edges of their fins wimpled softly in the flow. They smelled of moss in your hand. Polished and muscular and torsional. On their backs were vermiculate patterns that were maps of the world in its becoming. Maps and mazes. Of a thing which could not be put back. Not be made right again. In the deep glens where they lived all things were older than man and they hummed of mystery.

Cormac McCarthy, The Road

Why don't you write an anti-glacier book instead?

Kurt Vonnegut, Slaughterhouse-Five

II STRANGE ISLANDS

AUTHOR'S INTRODUCTION: A Hollow Book

To be honest with you from the beginning, this will end in bitterness. It will start however with the incomplete memory of a library, a school, and a book – and along the way, I hope it will contain wonders.

—

I think... but can't be certain... that it was my secondary school. I can remember the room. A large window revealed rooftops of other school buildings, so it must have been on the first or second floor. The glossy dark brown formica covered bookshelves, and pale varnished table tops. Stacks and rows of books through which I searched for adventures, and found, and devoured. I had a taste at the time for an ongoing series of books where two brothers would travel the world to capture rare animals for a zoo. But, the book I had on this particular day, was not from that collection.

I remember being sat on a plastic chair with the book, however I do not remember taking it from the shelves. The book had either: A plain blue hardcover, without a dust sheet, or a dust jacket with a single image. A black and white line-drawing of architectural spires – curved, bulbous. Perhaps it had both, or neither, such is the uncertainty of my memory. I cannot remember the author or title, for all my efforts. I have since occasionally tried to identify it, with no result. I would now prefer not to know.

What I can remember is how the book began and ended.

The book began with a child travelling to a relative's house, perhaps by car. This aunt, uncle, or grandparent, lived in a large house by the sea, a cliff top house. Once there, the child was left to themselves, or found their own space, away from the adults in the barely furnished rooms.

Then one night, the child receives a visitor at their open window. The visitor's eyes are too round, their limbs too long. They are something 'other'. The visitor would like to befriend the child, and offers them a tour of their world, they offer wonders and treasure. 'Just come down the narrow cliff path into the caves' they say, 'There is an entrance to my world'. This is the first chapter.

In chapter two, the child goes with the visitor, and, down the path and through the cave there is an entrance to their world. Perhaps underwater, perhaps not. But, everything they have offered is true. Their world really is full of wonders and treasures. The child is shown all of them…

I, on the other hand, cannot remember them. I only remember that there were spires, and colour, and light. Nothing else, I cannot remember the rest of the book, no other details, nothing except the ending…

After the journey, which takes some time, the child is magically returned on the same night as when they departed.

The visitor promises to return the next night, and then the child can leave with them to their world, forever, if they want to; and they do want to.

The next night however, the visitor does not come. So, the child scales the pathway themselves, and enters the cave, but the entrance is gone. Instead, they find a smooth cave surface, as if the opening had never been there. It is not a sealed entrance, nor an ordinary cave wall, it is just strange enough to let the child, and the child alone know, that the entrance had once been there, and is no longer.

H.G.Wells
Hole/ in the wall
door

The child's response to this blank refusal, took me by surprise. They were neither sad, nor mystified. They did not doubt the reality of the experience they had just had.

As I read the book, I realised that the child felt lied to, angry, and embittered. Their new friend was a fraud, a future had been stolen, a trust betrayed. The child undertook a long exhausting vigil of fury. They raged at the cave wall, screaming, and hurling rocks at it till they collapsed at its base. Then finally, on the closing page, the child makes their own promise, to counter the one discarded by the visitor. The kind of promise that is delivered with such commitment that it would reshape you with its utterance. They promise themselves that if they are ever to find a way into that other world again, then they would destroy it, and kill their former friend. Those are the final words of the book.

That is how I remember the ending of the children's book.

This book, the one that you have found (whose voice is currently in your head), this book is not my attempt to tell that lost story again or rewrite it. This book is written into the gap that my memory has left blank, like a homemade jigsaw piece for an incomplete puzzle. I am telling you this, as otherwise I think this book would make no sense, why else would someone compulsively imagine a series of islands, and attempt to create a space of wonders, cradled by bitterness.

VI   STRANGE ISLANDS

CONTENTS

Volume 5

Volume 6

Volume 7

Volume 8

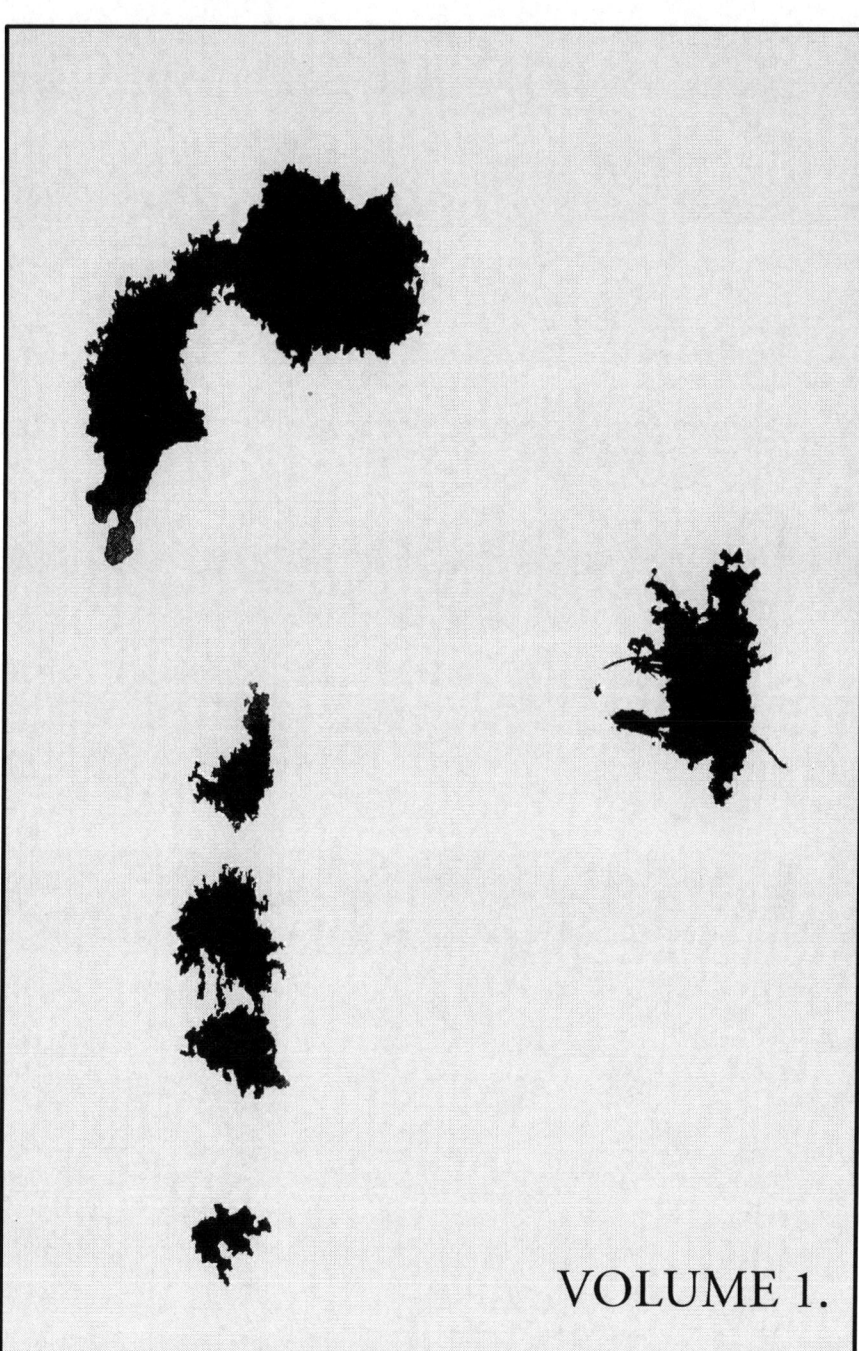

VOLUME 1.

A Fire at Sea.

There is a fire, at night, at sea.
Your boat is sinking.
Your eyes are burned.
Your body broken,
You are in the water, and cannot swim.
Drowning blind.

Even there, alone in all the oceans,
A boat is passing.
The Captain sees your pyre as signal flare,
They come to help.
They reach into the black waters,
Silvered by the Moon, gold-leaf applied by flame.
Grip your arm and hoist you,
Salvage on the deck.

You are sheltered and fed,
A slow recovery.
You have no place to go, they take you in.
And they go on, travelling from island to island,
A long journey.
Searching for something they don't disclose.

Each night they describe the island left behind.
They tell you its life, and unseeing, you write this in your mind.
You are now the map, the record, of a journey that isn't yours,
Of places you will never see, blind in someone else's boat.

Every time you wake you are panic stricken,
Pulled from sight.
You hurt.
Your body has been bandaged.

It's hard to move.
You find their frilled edges,
As you trace your fingers across your skin.
The bandages are wet,
A smoother texture over your skin,
Beneath which you can feel the wound.
The wound you know was inflicted by your burning falling mast,
The one you were trapped underneath.
The one that took your sight.

You can feel a cover over your body, a blanket.
You are lying on something soft,
A layer of something spongy.
As you lift your hand to your face it smells of moisture and soil.
You imagine you are on a bed of thick living moss.
You reach out around yourself,
Feeling out your close environment.
Fingertips quickly bumping into the physical world,
You visualise yourself in a wooden cot or bed,
Perhaps a shelf, low ceilinged, made of wood.
The wood is smooth to the touch,
Undulating like it has been cut from a tree,
But never properly finished.
You can feel the whorls and knots in the wood,
Patches of bark, rubbed smooth but not rubbed out,
You reach down to find a soft cool floor,
As you rake your fingers across the ground,
You realize that the floor of your cabin is covered in dirt.
Sticking under your nails, crumbling.
You push your fingers into it.
Beneath your fingers, you can feel roots,
A thin and tangled net.

For a moment everything your senses tell you,

Make you think that you are not at sea,
But rather on the ground itself, on an island.
But you can hear the creak of the ship around you.
You can feel the motion of it as it rises and falls on soft waves.
As you listen more intently,
You can hear the Captain moving on the deck above,
Light strides and operations being undertaken,
Ropes and pulleys being activated.
You can hear the sea,
Just beyond the wooden hull that encloses you
Splashing against the ship.
The two images collide in your mind,
That you are somehow both in the forest, while out at sea.
You drift back into sleep.

This is your world for a while; sleep, being fed by the Captain, and
listening to the ship.
When the Captain comes to you, you ask about your wounds and
what your bandages are made of,
'Seaweed' is the answer given.
Your bed is 'Moss',
which you find hard to understand how a bed of moss can be found
at sea.
You are told your body will recover, your eyes may or may not.

In the days and weeks that come,
You are able to lift your legs from the bed,
And place them in the dirt on the ground.
You ask the Captain, 'Why is there dirt in the cabin of your ship?'
The Captain says 'once it gets in, it never gets out'.
You ask about the roots,
To which the Captain cryptically replies that the ship is,
'Mostly a Tree, and the Tree can do what it wants'.
You ask what the rest of the ship is made of and the Captain says,

'The Sea',
~~Given that~~ your bed is actually moss,
You don't know what to think.

Each night, the Captain joins you in your cabin.
Feeds you, and checks on your recovery.
As she does, she talks:
'I would like you to remember something for me.
Let me tell you where I have been.
It is important that you remember the islands'.

VOLUME 1: ISLANDS.

Cliffs.

The first island the Captain tells you about appears different depending upon the direction from which you travel. The island either resembles a loose collection of paper, or at a distance, the teeth of a comb… becoming dominoes, becoming a queue of monoliths.

The island consists of a series of cliff faces each stood by the other. Perhaps once it was a single landmass that was chiseled away over years to produce the line of standing stones. There is no way to imagine that a series of separate cliffs could have been split from their original coastal homes, laid flat onto an army of barges, and floated here to be re-erected. But that is the myth, because that is the appearance; As each cliff varies in size and colour, inhabitants, and laws.

The cliffs are uniformly spaced, just wider than the reach of an adult's outstretched arms. It is easy enough to jump from one island to another, but far enough for there to be a lurching thrill with every jump, and enough accidents for the sight of a tumbling body to be in the memory of all.

The tides erode the foundations of the island, and while the majority of work undertaken by inhabitants is to maintain the foundations, the islands remain precarious. Visitors are plagued by nightmares of neighbouring cliffs tilting and crashing into theirs, and all cascading into a pile of rubble and foam. Islanders will migrate from cliff to cliff, season to season, depending upon where they feel safe. With this movement, few leave the island in their lifetime.

Grass grows on the top of every cliff, and so a population of Goats commands control of the cliff tops, with their shepherds as the elite of the island. Jointly they guard territory, bounding across the tops, herding their animals over the heads of those below. Those who seek the pleasure of laying on pasture, are beaten back down with measured force by wooden crooks, or worse, carelessly butted or kicked by the goats themselves.

The island prospers for its trade in dairy, meat and hide. Though few except the Shepherds profit, those below work on the foundations, and live there in exchange for a regular supply of food and shelter.

Mines.

Many islands are not as they appear, this island is gigantic but barely there at all. Some years ago, it was a solid mass of stone, a former mountaintop. It is still imposing above sea level. But the stone itself is a valuable resource; and so, the inhabitants have learned to mine. Over time they have sent shafts into its interior, first without planning or coordination; different groups each digging in their own lines. In addition to the stone they also hope for treasure. Perhaps gemstones, or a seam of gold at the heart of the mountain.

Now they have dug far below the surface, and the work is much more perilous. Each hammer strike comes with the risk of hitting a fault line that will lead to the ocean, a sea-strike, and the deeper they go the greater the pressure. Sea-strikes near the surface are just leaks that can be plugged with cork and tar. Sea-strikes at the lower depths are fatal lances of pressurised water, which can cut through flesh and bone, which cannot be stemmed, and only walled off with great risk and labour.

The population consists of only of two skill sets, the miners with delicate and precise excavation skills; And the surveyors, who dive into the waters outside the island, they measure their descent, and map the topology of the mountain with the length of their bodies against the silky green of its seaweed covered surface. Then they return and climb into the mountain's interior. Again, measuring the space with their bodies. They press themselves to its rough excavated void and give the miners their assessments. Here you can carve three bodies deep, here four, here just my arm. Here you can chip away my skin, and only my skin.

hollowing out — the island & themselves

In turn miners do not know the mountain anymore, they are the surrogate lovers of the surveyors. They touch the surveyors' bodies to know the mountain. Their excavations are gentle, slow. Over time their strikes have softened to become cuts, to become caresses, to become breath. The sound inside the island is of lovers whispering to each other, as bodies of stone leave the submerged mountain.

They know the island is finite. They know one day there will be a final catastrophic collapse, and that this will flood the interior and destabilise the entire brittle lattice. The island will vanish with a sigh.

Buoys.

No-one alive or in living memory has seen this island. No one ever will. No one is even sure there is an island, but there seems to be no other way to describe it. The location does not move with the tide, nor do its effects change by the weather or season. No one can get close enough, quickly enough, to see if it is there before dying. All that is known is that the area is contaminated, poisonous. It leaves no trace, but lifelessness. No sound, no smell, no taste, no sensation, but that of your own body dying.

Markers were left, a series of large buoys, set in three concentric circles. Each one can be seen with the naked eye from the other. The buoys of the outermost circle are set at a distance so that each one can be seen on the horizon. With each circle the distance between the buoys closes a little. They are painted different colours, with bells at the top that ring in the wind and swell. Yellow buoys mark the outer circle, and these are more elaborately adorned. Some with flags, written messages of warning, fearful imagery. Then the next circle, red with bells. Finally, the barely maintained black buoys, paint peeling, rusted, an often-silent rusted tongueless bell. Crossing the yellow boundary will make you sick in a matter of days, red within hours with a high chance of death. No one has returned from beyond the black markers alive. Occasionally a boat has drifted back out or through. Bodies rotting, the boats untouched.

There is a kind inhabitant here. Self-appointed guardians mark the outer limit in their boats, warning passers-by of the risk and how to navigate around it. They take the testimony of those who wish to pass across the black boundaries, narratives of despair and surrender. They caretaker the Buoys on the outer boundary. Occasionally they will attempt short trips to maintain buoys on the red boundary; if the bell ceases to toll, if it can be repainted. The most dedicated, will make their final trip to partially maintain an inner boundary buoy.

The guardians are sorrowful, because they are good people. The island is permanent they say, but the Buoys are not. One day the anchor chains will break, they say, the buoys will drift or sink. Then one day, no-one will remember why they were there. Without the buoys or the guardians, people will come and die. But, they have a greater fear. One day, people may come and survive, and find a way to the island. They imagine a future where the poison of the island is captured, and put to use, as a weapon. They say that because they can imagine this, it must come to pass.

Promises.

At night, the Captain ties knots.
Not to bind sails, but to pass time.
You hear the rope passing rough through her hands.
Till she passes them to you.

Not sailor's knots, but decorative ones,
loops and twists that mean nothing
unless you know their names.

She tells you: Globe Knot. Monkey's Fist. Friendship Knot.

When you ask her what they are for,
She says, "Every knot is a kind of promise. They are problems and
solutions at the same time."

Sometimes you wake with one tied loosely around your wrist.
You don't remember her doing it.
But you do remember dreaming of agreements.

Yachts.

They will never stop. White glimmering palaces on the move, driven by the sun. The yachts of the former world's wealthy, carrying on relentless. On board, perhaps the longest end-of-the-world-party, where entire lives are framed by the death of everything, and its denial. There are different ships, some track circles, some chase the day, some move from point-to-point. Birds do not travel in their wake, they leave no waste. They glide across the surface of the world, disdainful of its proximity.

Those that come near shore never dock, never close in, they rest on the horizon, presumably to see what is happening. The moment they are seen or approached, they are gone.

There must be Captains of these boats, crew. There must be passengers. None are seen. There must have been once, but now? Do the ships sail themselves, does a low hum speak of a serviced engine, or an automation?

There are stories of people being taken aboard; of children, the beautiful, the gifted being offered places. Their ships are rumoured gateways to another world, elevated, made ungraspable by smooth white hulls, by speed. These stories must be lies. No one shares a gilded coffin.

Long ago there were tales of ghost-ships; found in the dead calm, abandoned at a moment's notice. But those ships offered mysteries, beckoned you on board to ask what malignancy once stirred there. These ships withhold their secrets with great ostentation. They prowl through storms and puncture horizons. Great White Voids with polished sides that should not be looked upon.

Beaches.

It is never quite in the same place, occasionally not there at all, and never the same shape. Yet, the island is always instantly recognisable. It remains, mostly, under blue tropical skies, and is a rare golden streak on the horizon resolving into curves of yellow dunes. It might have been the high point of a Desert, it might be a remaining or newly formed sand bar. It is simply called The Beach.

On arrival The Beach is something of a child's dream, its central feature being a gigantic sandcastle under construction. This is the main residence of all inhabitants, the hub of all activity.

As the sand will not hold a complex shape, it must be simple, because of tide, and wear and tear it has to be constantly rebuilt, a building dissolving at one end and emerging at the other, a building erupting from the sea and sand.

Inhabitants are deeply tanned, sun bleached hair, exposed from childhood to the Sun, thin from a diet of fish.

Beyond the castle people walk the shoreline, they fish and search for flotsam and jetsam. Inland, smaller temporary dwellings are constructed, and children build miniature versions of the castle across the island, and create their own elaborate citadels, testing the limits of the sand.

In regular storms the castle is destroyed, and people huddle under blankets waiting for it to pass, and then a new building emerges, the new architecture never quite the same. Sometimes the blueprints are the designs offered by children.

When on occasion the tide rises, the inhabitants are swamped, sometimes up to their necks, a population of heads bobbing in the water. They grab hold of the grasses of the sand dunes between their toes to provide an anchor. Some break away and are never seen again. It is thought those who are taken, are taken by the sea for greater purpose.

Sometimes between the longest tides there is embellishment on constructions, there is refinement, and the lumpen masterpieces become ornate fingertip carved mysteries.

People are lured to the island by a dream of leisure and indolence, but life on the island is a constant toil of building, searching, fishing. Others come imagining that treasure is buried here, there is none. Despite there being other islands with rock and trees and beaches, it is the beach that these people turn to, digging vainly. The longer established inhabitants view these prospectors with scorn.

However, occasionally the living or the dead are washed ashore, and this event takes great significance. They are welcomed and honoured, everything that arrives by the will of the sea, is a gift to the island. That which arrives by design is to be distrusted.

Boards.

A trading island, built on the crumbled remnants of a long cliff face. Once a tall coastal line, now a rocky ridge. In its way beautiful, but unremarkable. There are many islands like this, collections of ramshackle house-of-card communities higgledy piggledy over the rocks. On the surface families and communities go about their meagre business. In support of this some piers are constructed at the forward edge, welcoming ships for trade. Under the piers another island reveals itself, of clandestine meetings, trades, bodies in the cool, wet dark. Slick seaweed, sharp barnacles, and human waste. Then further out into the tide and waves beneath the struts, driven by the swell of the ocean, other bodies move. Lean bodies, near naked, slip and crash their way among the posts, on sculpted wooden boards.

The island's shore is shaped in such a way that it gives way to a low angled slope into the sea, and this creates the ideal circumstances for long tall crumbling waves. There are strong tides and persistent winds from warm climates here too, all contributing to creating a relentless tumble to the shore.

And so just out to sea, as the tides dictate at sunrise and sunset, they can be seen. Scores of bodies silent, paused breathing on their boards, torsos in the ocean silhouetted by the sun, at sunset vanishing in the light. At a distance, as the swell rises and falls, they blink in and out of existence. They watch the sea, waiting for it to flex its body, to shrug off the pull of the moon, to shiver at the memory of a storm. When it does, the waves will come – rolling hills, limbs moving under dark silk sheets – and they paddle in front of them, choose one and let themselves be caught in its momentum, as a hand might guide a butterfly to a window. Then as the wave builds and the sea floor rises, the wave begins to peak, it makes its wall of glass for them to cut a path along, till the chaos of foam at the peak tumbles over and brings the wall down, spinning them underneath, between two horizons, to resurface dazzled, euphoric, breathless. They do not return to shore, they paddle out again to watch the sea.

When the morning winds have done their work, and waves no longer crest, they disappear, back to the island, through the day till evening-tide comes again. Just ordinary inhabitants of the island. Perhaps from the boats of the pier. But no one on the island knows who they are at that distance, no one asks on the island 'was that you I saw out there today'. You do not ask a person if they are a god.

Surfer gods

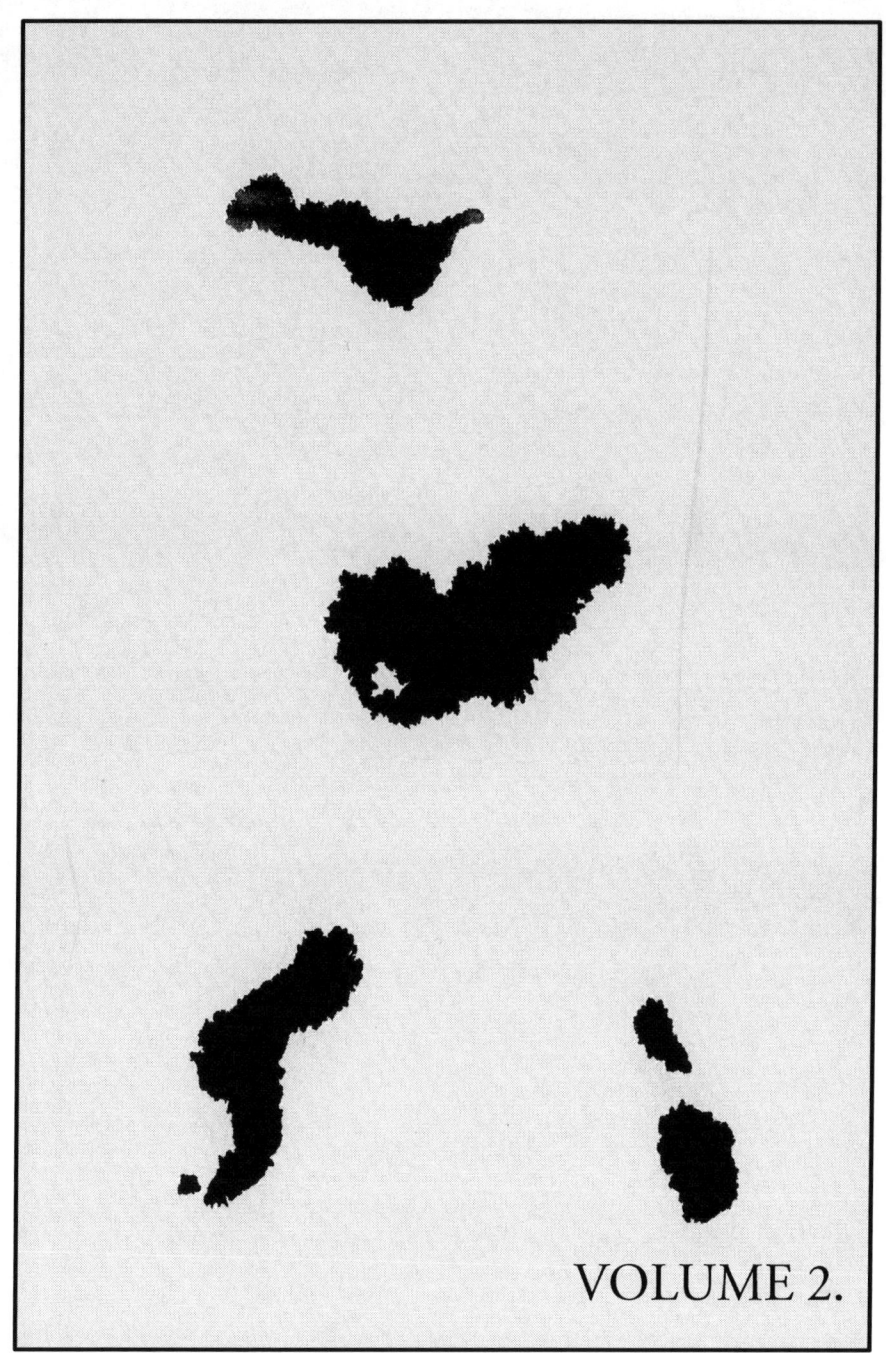

VOLUME 2.

The Map of a Flower.

Below decks. Wrapped in wood and seaweed.

The Screech and creak of pulleys and ropes being operated and the flapping of materials, undulations, resonant knocks.

'Rain' states the Captain entering your cabin.

You pause, 'I don't hear any'.

'Soon. It's almost on us. I'm going to make a flower'.

'A flower?'.

'For water collection… I reorganise the sails to create a frill around the edge of the ship, like leaves capturing the rain, it draws it in. I rearrange the main sails, tilt them out, curl them round, fluted like Lily. A rain flower. All the water flows in for collection'.

As the Captain talks, you imagine their hands conjuring a bloom.

'How do I know it actually looks like a flower?'.

'I could give you a more technical description if you'd prefer?'.

You think about what the Captain has told you so far about their travels.

'Your descriptions of the islands, they're not technical'.

There is a pause, the Captain leaves, returns, there is a soft brush of paper being unrolled and laid out on a surface, objects being moved.

'What are you doing?'

'Laying out some maps'.

For a moment your hands touch the Captains', they are small, slight,

captain made of paper

wrapped in fabric, something drier and coarser than your bandages. Your hands are delicately guided to a smooth flat surface, paper. You spread out your fingers, smooth, fine grain, near featureless to touch.

'I spend a great deal of my time navigating. I measure time, distance, speed, orientation. I note it all here. What can you tell me about where I've been, from what you feel?'.

You concentrate, you feel the surface of the paper, trace your fingers gently, searching for indentations, you find none.

'Nothing'.

'And yet it's all there, the facts are at your fingertips… but what sense will you make of them? How will anyone make sense of anything? There needs to be more… This is why what we discuss each night is vital. When I tell you about the islands, do you really want to know their measurements? Should I tell you how far they are from each other? Where they are? We have this already. Or would you prefer that we knew how each island feels, who the people are, and the shape and texture for their lives?'.

The rain begins to fall on the deck above. You listen, in the thicket of your senses the ship becomes a flower capturing the mist at the base of a waterfall.

'Tell me where else you have been?' you ask the Captain.

VOLUME 2: ISLANDS.

Crocodiles.

A thin and broken ragged line of emerald encrusts the horizon. An archipelago of the rarest of saltwater mangrove swamps. Its roots like fingers are buried into layers of silt, beneath them even deeper layers of silt. On what those layers lie, no-one really knows. The Monastic order that lives on the islands however, has a distinctive creation myth for their home. They believe the island rests on the back of a god, a god in the form of an immense crocodile.

The myth has its roots in cold blood and warm flesh, as amongst the knotted trunks and under the algaed waterline of the island resides a dense population of saltwater crocodiles. The adults are colossal, the length of three people sometimes longer. Ponderous when moving without motivation, but when triggered for food their reflexes are sprung traps, they are knives in the water, and territorially aggressive. Yet to the Monks they are the divine representatives of the god beneath, and worshiped accordingly by those who live in the canopy of the trees above.

Outsiders who do not know the island rarely survive if they enter the interior. Those who know the islands, do not enter. On occasion a passing boat has made the mistake of seeing a monk in the canopy and presuming them stranded, then approached to make a rescue. People will often make the strangest decision to approach a situation that they are being waved away from. If they set foot out of their boats, it is too late, they have been watched and followed from afar, by eyes that are inconsiderate of their motivations.

On the archipelago, the monks grow Orchids, grafted delicately into the tough mangrove bark, and cultivated beneath the canopy. In scattered light these pale fireworks unfurl, tended to by gentle hands; and there is a trade for these, beyond the island. They are the luxuries of the powerful; their gifts to lovers, emblems of excess. The austerity of the lives that tend them, is an authentic marker of their value to those with lives of plenty. A single orchid may provide for a monk for two years, and more for the island.

There is a further trade. The monks, though zealous in their care and protection of the crocodiles, are pragmatic when one dies. As the older creatures slow the monks can get closer, they tend to them, clean wounds and dirt from folds in the skin. They sing to the Crocodiles. Lullabies without words for ageing deities. Garlands of orchids are placed along their mountainous backs. But then, when the heartbeat stops, when the lungs are still, and the blood grows cold despite the sun – then the remains of the crocodile are lifted into the canopy with ropes made of root and vine and seaweed. The body is slowly turned till its belly faces the patterned sunlight breaking through the leaves. Then a knife of sharpened tooth, is slotted between the softer scales and is run from end to end. Its body is opened, and like a chandelier its innards are hung on branches over its emptied carcass. Its intestines are dried, organs salted, meat stripped from the inside out, soon the skin is harvested and stretched and cleaned for leather, bones are hollowed out and fashioned into a multitude of objects – functional, decorative and even musical; the teeth are blades, arrowheads, spear points. The toothless skulls, painted in the colours of the orchids, are held high on a row of poles, adorning the archipelago from end to end, above the ragged canopy.

They know the crocodiles individually, they are given the names of angels. They have raised them as guardians. Each breeding season the monks perch expectantly over the buried eggs. They are there to make sure each infant makes it into the water; that birds are kept away. They weep for lost infants and grieve the adult-dead.

The islanders collect their drinking water from the persistent rain, collected in the leaves of the uppermost canopy. They fashion long spears and pluck fish from besides the resting bodies and under the snouts of their demigods below. The monks eat only what they need, giving the majority of catches back to the crocodiles. In this way they build relationships of routine with them. The crocodiles know the monks in return, in their way, permitting them to descend and attend to their bodies. Monks can be seen reaching into their open mouths and picking rotting meat from between their teeth, garlanding their backs with orchids.

If these offerings are not made, then it is foretold that the crocodile beneath the island will wake with hunger, and begin to move and the whole island travelling with it as it does. This in of itself is not what the islanders fear. They fear that their hungry god will seek out a whale as easy prey, and when taking it in its jaws perform a death roll, spinning on its axis to incapacitate its prey. At that point, the island and the islanders and their world will be thrown apart and into the thrashing sea.

Sunken.

Denial is a powerful motive, it is the spirit of our age. The island appears as a short circular fortified tower emerging from the sea, capped by an elaborate canopy of mirrors and glass. But this is just the entrance. The tower descends from above the surface of the ocean, to the original city far below.

They thought they would hold back the sea, but they buried themselves instead. As the seas rose, so did the walls, buttressed from the inside against the pressure with great metal beams spiralling up the inside of the tower.

As such at the bottom, there is very little light. The canopy is their solution, it collects and redirects light from above the surface down into the tower. The inside of the tower is itself covered with a series of mirrors, and the inside of the wall panelled with polished and angled metal to circulate the light down to the city below. Each day they experience a distant and redirected sunrise and sunset, fragmented and played out over a thousand polished surfaces.

The Canopy protects the island from rainfall from above. While fresh water is essential, and only saltwater soaks the ground, its measured intake must be carefully managed for fear of flooding. As there is nowhere for water to go. There is also a complex vertical pulley system for the ejection of waste, and sewage, which is unfortunately prone to spilling onto the inhabitants below.

The inhabitants tell themselves every day that this was the best solution, that they did not have to move, and that the sea has been defeated by their ingenuity and determination. They are however at once terrified of, and reliant on, those from outside.

All their food must be brought to them, in exchange for their limited luxury crops of mushrooms and rhubarb.

They claim their tower is a marvel of engineering. It has, over recent years been protected by the deliberate seeding of forests of seaweed, by other nearby islands, who undertook it of themselves to prevent the catastrophic failure of the tower in the event of a tsunami.

Lighthouses.

To say that it is remote, does not go far enough. Our passage there was not deliberate not pleasant, storms and strange tides had thrown us off course, and so a long curving route had to be taken through cold dead seas before we were to arrive at somewhere that only served as a point to reset our journey. We passed this island one night.

The waters were a black mirror, the night sky clear, which made the first sighting of the island come early. A glow on the horizon, light shimmering and playing across the glass surface, tripped by ripples like a series of skimming stones thrown out in every direction. You think maybe you are approaching a floating city, till the light resolves from glitter into solid beams. The playful scatter becomes a cycle of interrogative lights.

It is hard to know what possible purpose of reason the island fulfils or how it came about, but it is impossible to miss. Eleven lighthouses of different designs and sizes all perched close together on a rocky outcrop.

The lights spin at different rates and heights, raking over the sea, sky and island. Though all, when pointing inward reveal the inner lighthouses. There is a point in their cannoning sequence, when all the lamps point inward, and the island is revealed entirely by direct light or by indirect reflection off the weathered white walls; the solitary largest central lighthouse alone in scanning the horizon. There are times when all the lights spin in two opposing circuits, and it feels like the island will be torn apart, such is the weight of the light that it feels like a physical force – wrenching at the foundations, pulling at the sky.

When one draws closer, what one might have mistaken for sun

bleached driftwood on the rocks is soon identified as the weatherbeaten remains of former keepers littering every surface. There are many heaps of crumbling bone; those that are fresh have seagulls gathering to pick at the flesh, and are swarming with crabs. The inhabitants are all keepers, they all end on the rocks. Each one arrives, scales the difficult cliffs, climbing over the bodies of former keepers. They arrive at a lighthouse whose door is currently untended, and knock. They wait there in silence, then in due course the keeper inside lets them in.

At night, outside the lighthouses, the island takes on an air of unreality. The lamps do not light the island directly, and the beams are tightly focused on the horizon, so only a little light descends, and a little more is refracted off the other towers as the beams pass. And so the eleven lamps animate the island like a zoetrope, each still and dead thing seeming to move as shadows of light move over them like a breath of life. In that world, the lighthouses themselves seem to shift in space, sometimes the boundaries of the island, like a slow and silent earthquake were taking place. The bodies of the dead keepers also seem to move. Skeletal remains look about and at themselves with amazement, the more recent dead shift about the ground as if uncomfortable on the ground they died upon. Only the sea around the island is still.

Each lighthouse has two rhythms, that of the rotation of the lamp, and that of the rotation of its occupants. On the ground floor the new keeper waits and paces the floor. Above them the second keeper climbs and descends the stairs. Finally at the top the final keeper keeps pace with the lamp, one step behind the light. There inside, on the ground floor they wait. The lighthouses glimmer wetly on the inside. There is a silvered sheen to the floor, the walls and every object touched, mercury. The lenses of the lamps of the lighthouses are floated in mercury, and there is a store in the basement of each lighthouse. It keeps the rotation smooth. The keepers carry it up the stairs regularly; it spills, drips, and is spread by touch around the interior, till everything has been gilded.

But the mercury brings sickness, blindness, and madness for the keepers and so up one level at a time, symptoms and illness accumulate.

The keeper of the lamp is always blind, a result of prolonged exposure to the mercury, and tends to lamp till by accident or design they fall or throw themselves from the tower. This is the lifecycle of the island, dead men climbing to their deaths after lives that hold nothing more for them.

Beyond the sound of the sea, the weather, the gulls and the barely audible crabs, there are seven sounds that are distinct to the island. The island seems silent, but these former sounds lay down a soft auditory blanket, but if one listens, one hears. There are the knocks that each keeper makes upon the door of the lighthouse they wish to enter; the pacing of feet upon the floors and stairs of each lighthouse; the slow oiled turning of the lamp; the fluttering of a falling keeper; the complex wet crack and thud of a landing body. These sounds are the dying heartbeat of the island.

But there is a seventh sound. A sound more felt at first than heard, then when first heard mistaken for a song of light, the guiding light from the lamps. But it is not, it is the siren's silence, the darkness that folds in behind the light that has cut it, that builds in a bow wave before it, that surrounds the island that forms the rocks on which the lighthouses stand. The light is the lure.

Stadium.

From above, it still looks like a stadium: oval-shaped, sloped, with rows of stone seats arcing around a central field. But no games are played here. Not anymore.

The island is a prison now. A prison for thinkers.

There are no cells. No guards. The prisoners arrive by boat, climb the outer stairs, and are left on the bleachers. They find others waiting—women, men, children, old philosophers, young dreamers, the mildly inconvenient. All labelled radical.

They live beneath the stands in rough quarters. But every day, they gather on the field to speak. They argue, debate, or simply listen.

Piers.

There is rock, and sand, but jutting out in every direction, overlapping and overreaching one another, pier after pier after pier. No central point, no plan. Perhaps once there was one pier, perhaps it was extended or adjoined. At some point a pier, ruined or dismantled or floated, was brought here. And then again and again. There are functional piers, jetties and docks, with boats and ships arriving, unloading, trading, reloading. There are leisure piers of residence and shops and amusement parks.

As one might imagine, the island of piers is constantly busy, with ships and boats of every size and kind departing at all hours, throughout the seasons. The piers themselves on the outer edge of the island have a moderate order, emerging radially from the centre to point in sixteen directions. Four cardinal points of North South East and West and then all those in between. The angles however are not quite right, more indicative than true. Indeed the size and quality of the piers also speaks to this imprecision. While the Pier for North is a large solidly built arm pointing defiantly into the cold, South is an uneven grin of thin rotting skeletal boards that meanders only a few hundred feet before disintegrating.

The interior of the island is stranger still, a spiralling stack of piers built atop a buried and barnacle encrusted rocky outcrop that barely breaches the surface. They sit and overlap in every direction, like a badly shuffled deck of cards, like a piano smashed by a boulder.

The island, one would presume, makes its living from trade. This is not the case. Each Pier is a theatre, and the true inhabitants of the island, a band of players for hire. Their speciality is to convey meaning to a journey. Each Pier is lit and dressed, and every arrival and departure is attended to by a team of performers who can give your journey the meaning you require. If you can afford it. Simple plays involve a tearful farewell from a family, or passionate clinch with a lover. Otherwise a cluster of trading partners in fine attire can follow your departure, or await your return. A last minute escape from criminals or authorities, a clandestine but conspicuous meeting of spies, a kidnap, all can be arranged. Sometimes all that is required is a priest for a prayer, or a friend for a warm welcome. What is paid for is the manifestation of a hope, or the consolation of a lie.

At night the island is twice as busy and plunged into darkness. Piers are closed and illuminated by a solitary ghost light. These manage the whispered arrivals and departures, of those who have not yet paid for a performance, or are leaving after an arrival.

Also at night silent rehearsals are staged. Choreographies of grief and joy, dumbshows of arguments and deals, all jostle on crowded boards for an opportunity to be refined or tested in the open air. The crowds of performers, in role, assess each other from the corners of their eyes. Whose mourning routine is the most authentic, which stowaway the most graceful. They return to cool lodgings beneath the piers to briefly sleep before the early dawn of optimistic voyages.

Flags.

For outsiders of a certain kind, the island is the centre of the world. They travel from their own islands as envoys to meet with their counterparts from other islands to discuss matters of trade, boundaries, alliances and disputes. They practise diplomacy. And so they come on their finest ships with the flag of their island flown high, large, and of the boldest colours. They expect to see themselves represented on the island as well, they all do, and this shapes the island and its inhabitants in far reaching ways.

The island is a solid unforgiving grey slate, a smooth flat surface that emerges from the sea towards the sky sloping up till it breaks off to leave a ragged cliff behind which a barren rocky coast has formed. However, this is not what you see on the approach. The smooth back of the island is punctured by tens of tall weathered flag poles, each carrying the flag of a remote island nation. Every colour, a flurry of competing designs, but all the same rectangle and size. The island is an old spiny backed creature, one that has made its way through a meadow of flowers and speared every blossom it was possible to capture. Now the field floats above the island at a distance rolling in the wind, gleaming in the sun.

The visiting ships drop anchor and small boats row ashore and dignitaries arrive and raise a flag on an unoccupied pole. They greet other dignitaries beneath them, and after complimenting the flags, gifts are exchanged, and agendas set out.

The flag has become the means of assessing the wealth, power and culture of an island. To serve this display, the inhabitants of the island play an important role. They make, and maintain the flags. As such they are not only paid in food and resources, as nothing grows or lives on the rock, but also they are brought the fine threads and materials to do the work.

Those envoys that bring the best of these, have the finest flags. Those that cannot, their flags and therefore their nations are poorer, duller, and of less note. Those that bring nothing, the flags are neglected, ripped, and soiled, before being pulled from their masts by the elements, and forgotten. Tatters blown and drifting up the slope and off the cliff.

So, beneath the poles, huddled in thick hides, and heavy wools, the inhabitants under makeshift leather shelters, needle and cut away, faces and bodies wrapped tight. Just rough calloused hands emerging to work materials, day in and day out for their paymasters.

But largely they support a lie. Many dignitaries have little to offer from their island to another one, and their islands are rarely described accurately. The flag hides the reality of each island, and all know it. An island may be rich in a resource, but have no effective way to transport them over a distance, or have no cloth to bring. Many envoys make deals with islands that cannot be fulfilled, with both parties well aware. Others come to collect a flag as proof, and report back only lies. It is suspected that some ships are of no nation, no island at all. Unwilling nomads who circle to and from the island, with nowhere else to go, using it as a means to identify those that can be stolen from or deceived. The envoys stand on the decks of their ships as they slowly sink, beneath their flags as they fray.

All this time the needles work, the eyes of apprentices straining in low light, with their master's eyes barely glancing at the work, their hands feel the way with precision. At the end of the day they quietly make their way to the top of the island, and slowly climb down the cliff to the shore where their weather beaten town of tents is pitched low against the wind, tents connected by tiny canvas crawl tunnels into which they disappear till morning. They carry with them the rags of the day, the off cuts and left over threads.

Inside a multitude of other worlds await, softly hidden from the world outside. Stitched together with a level of care far beyond their work on the flags, is every reclaimed piece of material. Here their work continues, in the production of private luxuries, and the necessities of life.

Each rugged tent is on the inside a lovingly crafted room. The materials are not thrown together, but curated, so as to make one coherent world after another.

You can tumble from a pocket of cerulean blue, adorned with golden patch stars, into a tangle of soft silk roots canopied by layers of green mesh; on again into wide open red warmth, a discarded flagpole holding up the vault of a circus tent cathedral.

Intricate arrangements heighten every texture, rough or hard materials set in silks or deep corduroys.

Across surfaces caravans of buttons parade single file across the undulating hills of the fabric then mushroom in clusters arranged for tactile pleasure. The buttons are fashioned from different materials; bone, metal, wood and plastic; into a variety of shapes, geometric, abstract and figurative. You may find a hand carved wooden cat button, or a clay human face. That or buttons made from old objects retaining their shape, key as button, coin as button. If tested some buttons open pockets, or hidden folds that are doorways to other chambers.

And so the hidden woven city goes with the inhabitants living in a luxury provided by their labour. They undress and spend their time naked in their creation, warm pale soft skin on the fabrics, only their weathered hands revealing their link to the outside world, ever busy on the beauty of the interior.

The needle finds other surfaces to work on as well, as on some inhabitants it leaves its trace. Rather than tattoo, with the finest needles and softest threads their bodies are embroidered. Lines and patterns of colour weave along limbs, small heaps of thread allow for a series of buttons to be anchored, or light materials fixed. Gossamer wings, second skins, velveteen pockets, and hand-made furs adorn.

The rich diversity and complexity of their culture is unseen by the world, they do not hide, but few have sought to enquire of their lives. Those that have, for whatever reason have not revealed their secret, or have simply never left the island, and taken up the needle.

Whispers.

The Captain told you the moss in your cabin was self-aware.
That it needed your breath, more than light.
You asked if it would grow.
She said, "Only if you speak to it."

So one night, you did.
Whispered into the roots beneath your bunk.

The next morning,
you are sure that the air in your room,
has been purified.
Had it replied?

Grass.

It's just a field of grass.

It's just a field of grass.
A picket fence,
A low mist,
Dew in the mornings,
The sun a silver coin in the sky,
There's nothing else,
Perhaps, occasionally, you might think you see wild hare,
Amber eyes in the distance.
It will always be gone before you are certain.
There's nothing but grass, verdant and thick,
A spider,
A bat,
Flies, beetles, bugs.

No one steps foot on it.
It's easily circumnavigated,

Easily located,
Everyone knows where it is,
Anyone who cares to have seen it has done so.

Its size is precisely measured.

But with the mist, it is just big enough to never see the far side.

You can spend a few hours going round to see it all,
But never see it all in one go.

But no one has stepped foot on it.

People imagine a grounds keeper.

There is work being done, a game being played, a process.

It is holy.

At most, in passing, a traveler has reached out from the deck of their vessel, and with the barest of fingertips felt the softest cut of a single blade.

It's just a field of grass.

VOLUME 3.

The Sky and the Sea.

Eventually you can move yourself from your cabin, while the Captain does not wish you to roam carelessly around the ship, they escort you onto deck some days.

Today you are on the deck, a sky so blue you do not need to see it, so blue can feel it on your skin. You feel around, you cannot be certain, but some surfaces feel less like wood and more like stone or coral, or sometimes smooth in one direction and rough in another, like the skin of a shark or fish, ropes feel like sinew or muscle.

You tell yourself, that as you have lost your sight your other senses are not heightened, but they are trying to fill the gap left by vision, and to be doubted. Or perhaps what your eyes told you was never quite what the rope was to begin with, and who knows what the Captain makes ropes from.

The Captain is navigating. You ask how they navigate the seas since the world broke.

'Did you ever see glass?'.

'Yes, in the ruins of a building'.

'Good, imagine a cloud of glass floating in the sky. Flat sheets of glass suspended together. Different shapes and sizes… Where each pane of glass meets another, they do not break, or even touch, they pass through each other, like ghosts. They intersect with others at different angles, and just pass through each other… Circulating. The sheets of glass are the oceans. Each one is its own world… The coordinates haven't changed, North is still North, but over time I might take the ship North and cross into an ocean that used to be West, and then turn East and find an island that was South.'

'Some edges are safe to navigate, and the borders are easy to spot, a

line in the ocean and the sky, a shift in tide and stars, the heat of the air… But in other places, the intersection is a storm. I have to line up the ship alongside the edge, wait for the waters to align, time the moment of crossing precisely, have the ship rigged, for two completely different sets of conditions.'

'That's why I've kept you below decks, you've felt the ship lurch?… This is why hardly any islands have sustained contact with another, either the seas are moving or the crossings are too high risk… This is why the islands are the way they are, it's as if you were reading a book, and you understand the language, and you know what kind of story it is, but the pages keep reordering themselves, and once in a while you come across a page from an entirely different book'.

You pause, and ask 'Did the people from your island have a story about what happened to the world?'

'My island?… No, my island had no explanations for anything'.

VOLUME 3: ISLANDS.

Inferno.

The ash-white tower of smoke rises from the island undisturbed by offshore breezes till it meets the slowly churning cloud of lightning above. Lower down at the horizon the air ripples above the ocean because of the immense heat given off by the island. Closer still, one cannot approach, the sea itself boils, steam rising at points obscuring the island. The sea itself is so unstable that the boats will sink, losing buoyancy, killing mariners with brutal efficiency as shrieks of horror are cut short.

With a lens one can see the island itself, a cracked and crusted dome, the smoke relentlessly purging from its highest point, feeding the cloud above which reciprocates with regular violent whips of lightning. From the cracks in the dome flames emerge, and roll across the surface of the island. No one knows the source of the fire and smoke, it may simply be geological. There are enough fires in the world that the island would be unremarkable and worth neither visit, nor mention except, the island is inhabited.

There are not many, perhaps only seven charred figures. They emerge from the smoke, moving awkwardly and stiff-limbed, like each dried muscle is pulling in a different direction. They are naked, any clothes long since burned away, if there ever were any. But any modesty is pointless, they are remnants, just the glowing embers of people. The fat has rendered off each body, but skin and muscle has refused the shed, instead it has hardened over the bones which still show through the occasional crack. There is no hair, little way to sex them bar size, no way to determine age or ethnicity. And yet each one remains constantly, impossibly, moving and on fire. As they walk hollow socketed about the isle, something of them burns, and gives off flames.

One is small, and is assumed to be a child.

For the most part they wander alone without purpose. They do nothing functional. Occasionally they seem to scan the horizon, and if they see a ship (how they do this without eyes no one can guess), they are enraged. They stagger to the shoreline, flail their arms, their mouths snap open-and-closed, clicking fire-bleached teeth. They turn to each other and gather, mimicking the acts of screaming and shouting at the distant ship. No air escapes their mouths. So then they claw at the blackened surface of the island and hurl it into the sea in a futile but demonstrative act. They will go so far as to dip their feet in the sea, sending up plumes of steam, forcing a retreat. Such is the heat contained within their bodies.

There is no mistaking their actions, even though there is no explanation for them, these are not gestures of desperation, nor warnings. Their frames cradle an inferno of hate, and it does not die.

Stilts.

It seems to float in the sky; An inverted pyramid of dwellings, as if the island had been sliced off the surface of the sea and flipped to regard itself, like narcissus and his reflection. But in its shadow, one can see something less magical, but no less remarkable, as the island is balanced on hundreds of stilts reaching down to the sea floor. The stilts are thin, flexible, but essentially strong constructions of varying materials.

Like a sea urchin, walking on its spines, they are individually lifted, repositioned and tested, then secured before the next is moved. But as the island is supported by so many, enough are in motion to make it appear that all are moving in a great ceaseless search for firm foundations. As the island progresses on its way the stilts are relocated, or given maintenance by being lifted out to the side or above the island. So a great array of stilts wave gently in the air around the city, radiating out. When seen in full sunlight the island resembles an exploding star, and when silhouetted at sunset or sunrise a terrifying negative of the same image, an implosion into a black hole. At night, with the city lit and the stilts illuminated at various points by hanging lamps to aid their maneuvers, the island becomes a constellation in slow procession, like the magi wandering on the horizon.

The lives of those on the island are divided into shifts, all sharing in the task of keeping the island aloft. One shift works the stilts – lifting, relocating, securing with care; another shift is maintenance and construction; another shift is work; the final shift is rest and sleep. The work of the island is the hunting of fish and game; given the islanders skill with the stilts, harpoons both for air and sea are the favoured method.

The story the islanders tell is that the island was just like any other, and as the seas rose, the inhabitants rather than leaving, moved inland and built upwards. Soon they were building on top of each other towards a central high point that became an uncoordinated tower, hurriedly stacking upward until it began to be unsafe. The whole thing may have come down, but at some point, someone realised that instead of going ever more vertiginously up, they could go out sideways. Above the island below. And so they did, projecting out from the side of the tower, and pushing down a strut to take the weight. Once others saw that it could be done, the island mushroomed up and out unfurling from its stalk. Once the struts were in place, the stalk was cut, and the island was free.

On the gigantic flat upper surface of the island, the stilts are managed and birds are hunted. It is a flat panelled expanse of different colours, weather worn and full of sleeping bodies. As most of the islanders work inside, when at rest they come to the top to sleep. Around them children play, running and devising games around reclining adult bodies. Teenagers loiter at the edges, and construct small dips in the surface to remain in the light but evade observation. Up there is also no other world, it is just the island and the horizon. It drifts through clouds and even the waters are absent.

Celestial.

The ocean swells into permanent hills and valleys, with concentric circles of ripples running up their sides towards their summits like the gradient lines on a map. Incoming storms into the region are calmed, clouds are whipped away like a silk cloth from the top of a polished table. The waves calm themselves as if slowing in awe of what they approach. Transit through this area is swift if navigated through the lowest valleys in an undulating sidewind using the lowest slopes for momentum. However, do not sail to the top of any hill, or gravity will take you or your ship.

Suspended unnaturally over the ocean, low, a few miles up, are a series of celestial wonders. A moon, a dozen planets with an asteroid belt weaving between them, a small red sun, a rocky planet with a ring of ice particles, a strange spinning star that emits a beam of light in lighthouse fashion, and a lightless sphere of void, surrounded by a flat circle of burning plasma.

They are smaller than they should be, but remain gigantic in the sky. They should not be able to pause there without structure or means to do so, but they do; Pulling on the ocean, in tantalising reach of all those below.

One of the lowest moons is a reminder of the risk of approach. Light ships having sailed to the summit of the sea swell beneath were simply lifted. They slip through the fingers of the ocean, and fall upwards to spin and turn and crash catastrophically into the hard indifferent grey rock of the moon above. From the sea below we look up at the shipwrecks normally obscured to us, and they remain preserved without decay. With a telescope the details are held in time – shattered masts, crushed hulls, cargoes spilt, the bodies of sailors frail and broken clinging to ropes, impaled on the splinters of beams, or pasted to the surface like flies crushed against a wall, awkward creases in their clothes, strange folds in their bodies never to be corrected.

This warning only cautioned us, as such wonders have a gravity all their own. So you can make port here on the ocean swells, one ties ones ship to circular piers running the circumference. These rotate, rise and slowly fall, taking ships and releasing them in a gentle slingshot. The motion of the piers is created by the people who come to see the celestial sights, and walk in circles beneath them looking up. Everyone who docks walks in the same direction, never leaving the place they first set foot, with the walkway moving beneath them. As visitors come and go, the balance of weight is shifted and the walkway tilts to create rises and falls in their Sisyphean wanderings. They regard and walk towards the wonder, never really moving, and when finally tired they board their ships, to stop walking and begin to move away.

Storm.

She did not wake you.

The ship was already leaning when you stirred,
not rocking, but bowing.

A relentless pressure.

Rain had found the cracks.
You felt it on your wrists, your throat, your eyes.

Above, everything screamed:
the rigging, the hull, the sky.

The storm took an eternity to pass.

Later, you asked why she hadn't called for help.
She said, 'You were the most fragile thing on the ship.'

Trust.

In some respects the island looks like many others you will find, a jumble of buildings on a high point. But closer inspection reveals two notable differences. First of all, a lack of ships. Most islands are surrounded by fishing boats and the coming and of visitors, but neither are present here. But closer observation still, with the details of the construction of the island becoming visible, something peculiar is revealed.

A rusted tower, a rope bridge, a narrow archway, a grand staircase, a column, the stones of a public square, a brick wall, a small churchside fountain, a sash window, a revolving door, a Cathedral's Gargoyle, a stone built cottage, a stained glass window, the underside of a motorway overpass, a tiled fireplace, a railway platform, a drawbridge, a lighthouse's spiral staircase, a weathered windmill, a secret garden gate.

The architecture of the island makes no sense, it is a combination of a host of very specific buildings and details, none of which belong together. What an islander will tell you is that at some point one of the buildings here was deemed worthy of either historic or aesthetic value to require preservation. What is unclear is whether that particular building was moved here, or another was moved to this site to join it. But soon enough that is what the island became, a location to bring buildings and architecture of note for the purpose of preservation.

A mausoleum's entrance, a gothic balcony, a clock tower face, a stone-carved bench, a majestic palace entrance, a watermill wheel, a crumbling castle turret, a moss-covered stone circle, a Roman aqueduct arch, a Zen garden's stepping stones, a Corinthian column, a dilapidated barn door, a pagoda's intricate roof tiles, an ancient amphitheater seat, a castle courtyard well.

There is a chance the whole thing is a sham, someone might have simply declared their building, or a range of buildings, as important, perhaps even relocated them for show. If someone arrived having moved an entire building across an ocean would you doubt their authenticity.

A seaside cliff staircase, a mountain path rock steps, a city park chess table, a cryptic monolith, a garden's decorative tilework, a market square fountain, a mission bell, a castle's portcullis, a wrought-iron fence, a boulevard streetlamp, a log cabin chimney.

And why would they lie? It serves no purpose, there is no profit. The whole island is a testament to trust. As the island is inhabited by those who brought the buildings here, and with windows drawn, they preserve their allocated building. Visitors are permitted, and walk designated pathways. While the attendants wait cautiously for either an outreached hand to chide, or an unsuspecting question allowing them to launch into monologues of history and knowledge.

A bridge iron railing, a public art sculpture, a stone marker from a mountainside, a villa terrace, a market stall, a chimneystack, a subway station mosaic, an Egyptian pyramid chamber entrance, a carnival carousel base, a chipped street curbstone, a hammock post.

The island is a collection, a bricolage of salvaged buildings and their fragments. What is strange is that there is no life here, that the preservation is so absolute that a kind of death has taken residence as well. There are no children, no work, no trade, no leisure, no thought or investigation. The trust given to each building and its attendant becomes a shackle.

Plastic.

There are many islands such as this, it forms a bulk of what has come after, made from what was left over from before. A dirty, colourful, disintegrating but never fully disappearing mass of plastic. You know you are down-wind of one such island from fragments of bags and sheeting filling the air like a swarm of fake butterflies. Down tide, miniature islands pass by, microcosms of what you are about to encounter. Mists of pale rainbow plastic dust on the horizon.

It is a landscape that mocks one of natural beauty, with sad awareness of its own limitations. A great mound and scattered hills, rolling down to the sea, a flat plain of fragments swirling on the surface.

The island is adrift, nearly all of them are. They could be sailed if they were not so ungainly and unstable. A few stories persist of ships attempting to tow them. Large ships frustrated by the tendency of the island to fragment. Small ships dragged underwater when pulled by the weight of this ersatz iceberg tilting and rotating to present a new side to the sun.

The plastic simply does not behave, or rather it does what any material does, decays. What had thought to have been distinct from 'nature' above it, beyond it, was soon dismissed by it. Life evolved to incorporate, consume and then disregard it as a laboursome material.

Crabs scuttle about the island, stacked high with crustacean shells interwoven with curls and loops and layers of 20th century packaging. Bacteria have formed to eat it, across the island there are patches, where the surface is a slick blue green. There are concentric circles dipping Into the mass of the island and expanding across its surface, like ripples that glacially peel and consume the island.

The natives of the island have been there a long time. Short term visitors will choke on the dust, making it past and through any filter that can be fixed to face. The natives have evolved like the crabs to accommodate and absorb the plastic. Their rib cages have parted down their backs, their lungs rising to the surface, and pores in the skin have enlarged to act as valves, that on breathing-out more effectively expel the oily film of flecks. They too though, like the crabs, are being overwhelmed by the sheer volume and invasive propensity of the material. From pores to orifices, and cuts or folds in skin the plastic finds its way in. Wounds sprout treelike fragments standing proud from a bloody healing root. Faces are cruelly ornamented with frills in eyelids, fragments woven into hair, threads between the teeth and layers under thin expressive skin. For each body soon the mass of plastic overwhelms the flesh, it weaves through every bone and organ, round each cluster of nerves, till something chokes, or blocks, and then the body stops. Or if it finds a way to carry on, the bacteria begins its work, and soon the thicket of plastic weeds invading the body is being eaten, and the body finds that its own structure long being compromised, was being held together by the plastic. A native of the island may be standing one moment, till some small microbe works its way through some accidental connecting thread, and like a net full of fish it cuts loose what holds the imagined whole together, and a sudden messy unraveling occurs. Leaving nothing but a tangled heap for crabs to feast and pick on.

The work of the island, its value to others, is the excavation of worthwhile plastics from the mass, the management of the bacteria in consuming the waste, and the farming of Crabs, for their meat. As the islands roll through the oceans, they capture the drifting plastic of the past, the people of the past, and redistribute it as crabmeat for the future.

Revenants.

'You sound angry when you talk about the ruins out there.'

You say it without blame. Just observation. Her voice shifts when she speaks of certain places — harder edges, brittle pauses.

She laughs, but it's not joy. 'I've sailed through rain that smells like bleach and burning. Seen whales with bellies full of the waste of the old world.'

You listen.

'I've watched coral cities bleach like old paper. Schools of fish suffocate in poisoned tides. Islands where nothing grows now, not even lichen. Where the water tastes of iron and forgetting.'

The ship rocks gently beneath you. 'You still go on,' you say.

'Someone has to chart them,' she replies. 'Even if they're ugly. Even if they make you sick.'

You imagine these places — bleached and broken, filled with plastic bones and oily tides.

Islands that were never meant to last, and yet, still remain.

'Some islands are full of ghosts,' she says. 'And I'm not always sure which kind.'

'The ghosts of those who lived there?'

'Or the ones who made them like that.'

Pearl.

The island has two halves, two names, two folk. To outsiders it is called The Wave, and the name is entirely appropriate. If I ask you to imagine an ocean wave reaching the shore, rising as it glides effortlessly, its back a perfect curve, the sun catching the miniature fractal ripples on its surface to produce a myriad of glittering white accents, which only make the wave itself seem both darker and bluer than anything else has been before, accents which conjure the weight and power of the wave to its surface, till suddenly it is rising to a point when those shards of light coalesce and a line is formed, the line becomes the foam and the froth of the crest of the wave as it leans forward in its momentum, changing from one curve to two, one at its back driving it forward, and the curve at its front, reaching up like a scythe before the sun, readying to come down, and in that moment the water is rushing and surging, but also pure, untroubled, smooth, and just clear enough to let the light through so that it becomes a single pane of a stained glass window, cerulean at peak and cetacean at the base... Imagine that wave, some 200 feet high, some 800 meters across, frozen solid, frozen in time, its muscular back topped with snow, and a small community of people living there in huts and tents. That is the appearance of the island of The Wave, at a distance.

Yet that is only half of the island; the half that is most apparent. In the shadow of the wave, beneath its crest, a flat rocky expanse opens up, and steam rises from it. Here people live among the warm water springs that stop the wave from encroaching further. Water drips down in steady streams from the peak, gathered with some care from those below in case of falling ice. Their homes – tents and huts, small aggregations of cuboid strangers – set back underneath the protective outstretched hand above them. And at the meeting of ice and stone at the base of the wave, if one were to look deep into the ice, you would understand why islanders have their own name for their home, they call it the Oyster.

Level with the rocky foundation, but set far back into the ice is a colossal shadow, a dark object at rest at the core of the island; And they call this the pearl. They believe that whatever it is, it was deserted, washed up, or discarded, on the far shore, and as waters rose and froze, they froze around it, and like a pearl around a grain of sand, the island formed, till it reached the warmth of the springs. The entirety of the island is as a result of this slumbering mass entombed inside the edifice of ice.

Of course there is an urge to discover what the pearl is, to excavate into the ice, tunnel and discover what... a buried building or community, a long forgotten submersible craft beached, the frozen remains of a deep sea leviathan brought to surface... any of these could be the grit around which the pearl coalesced. The idea of what it could be perhaps more tantalising than its reality. An island formed in the shadow of a sea monster, or a strange craft is greater than the flesh or steel of the thing itself.

This is tempered by another intrusive reality, that to dig into the frozen wave, might weaken it, might create fractures that could extend up into the body of the wave and in an instant bring the frozen blue sky above them bouldering down into crushing death.

And so the story of the island's origin, its myth, its future is held incomplete. The pearl cannot be known, and so stories layer around it like the ice. Except for the intervention of children.

There are fissures in the wave, natural ravines, formed as water trickles down, as warm earth gently pulls at the ice from underneath. Small. Say half an adults' height, say half an adults' width, but not too small that a child could not work their way into them, sliding back in time through the ice towards the mystery at its centre. No chiselling or cutting, to make a wider path. A negotiation with the wave itself. And so children's natural curiosity and diminutive scale are put to use. Each child is encouraged as a rite of passage to explore the paths that lead into the ice. Wrapped in thin layers to keep them warm, tied to ropes to help pull them back, they are ceremonially dispatched to explore and report on what they can see. Each child chooses their point of entry, and progresses as far as they can for as long as they can. To press their bodies into the narrowing and darkening spaces, to gaze as their blood cools deeper into the past of the island, to look for shapes and shadows, outline and clues, to feel for tremors, to listen to the low creaks and high vibrations of the water that is not truly still... but rather immeasurably slow.

Some children are lost. They are pulled back and having let the wave take them for too long have frozen and slept and not returned. Some are lost, the rope is pulled back, but without a child... sometimes the rope has frayed, or a badly made knot, intentionally or not, has come loose, and in those circumstances the child is never recovered, but is heard talking and crying before they fall asleep. The community gathers – They speak to them, they sing to them, fires are lit to give the child light. When a child is lost in such a way, the fissure is sealed, packed with the purest snow from the crest of the wave. They are additions to the foundations of the island and its solidity, pearls in miniature.

Finally there are children who find a ravine and enter, and keep travelling and progressing deeper, the rope pulls and extends, slowly at first, but then there is a sudden ease and hastening. As if the child has found not a crack but a pathway or a space, and begun to walk at speed. The child will be too far at this point to be called for, parents may shout after them, but the ravine is too narrow and convoluted to carry a voice coherently. They may tug and pull at the rope, or even try to hold it. But it will continue till the rope runs out and disappears forlornly after its leader into the dark.

These children never return, their ravines never explored again, and never sealed, till the movements of the earth and ice seal them naturally. A name is carved into the ice at the entrance. A small list of names runs along the surface of the wave. Their names are sung to children as lullabies.

As for the many children who return from exploring the ice. They most often tell experiences of hearing the voices of children emerging from the ice, and seeing shadows in the ice that may be the frozen bodies of their predecessors. As they explore they pass a child lost some weeks ago, or some decades ago. They report distant movements, and the outlines of pathways and chambers that are inaccessible. But none can report on the pearl itself, which remains ever shrouded and distant. It is these words and experience of children in cold dark cerulean spaces that preserve and carry forward the myth of the island. Wide eyes looking deep into ice for revelations and discoveries.

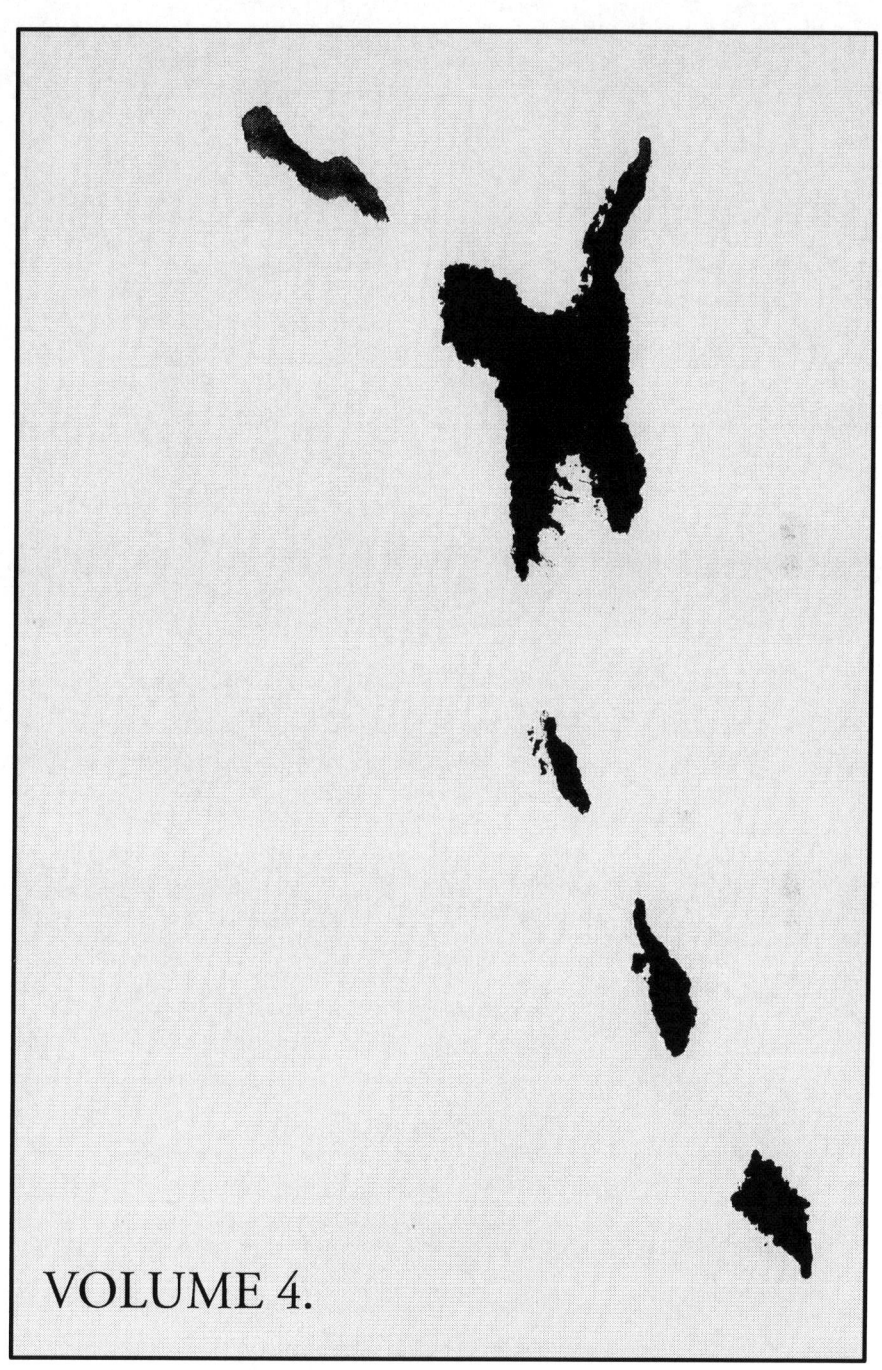

VOLUME 4.

Doubt.

You worry for a long time,

If the Captain is lying about the islands you have visited.

Do they really exist?

What if there were no other islands – just adrift, or sailing you around the same island, and we were stopping at different docks, and describing a different aspect of the same thing.

Then she brings you on deck,

And you can hear the islands,

Smell them.

Then she brings people on deck from islands to meet you, to talk to you. For you to tell them about the islands you've visited.

They place objects in your hands,
Fabrics, tools, jewellery, delicacies, resources.
The world starts to become real because it becomes tactile, and because the objects have history.

But after you have shared stories and treasures,
Away from the Captain,
In hushed tones they ask you other questions:

'Is the Captain bandaged because they are scarred?'.
'Is the ship alive?'.

'Is the Captain on the run from the island she escaped from?'...
'Or is the Captain hunting something?'.

They ask if the islands you have been to are real.
You begin to trust the world is real,
Because the others in it doubt it too.

So you trade stories and explanations
For how the world came to be the way it is.

The earth cracked from the inside out.
God broke the universe, on purpose.
God dropped the universe, by accident.
We did something, and ruined it.

The Captain has listened to all these theories,
And one day interrupts your collection of explanations.

'The story of the past is simple.
Nothing went wrong.
Nothing new happened.
It just happened.
This is how the universe actually works.

Everyone always imagined that all of this was... stable and
coherent,
That the way it was, was the way it always would be.
Because that's all we could remember.

But, all those millennia...
Just a fraction of the vast expanses of time,
A fraction of how the universe actually works,
Then simply...

There were cracks in the sky,
Cracks in the sea,
Cracks in the earth.
With the cracks came the waters,
with the waters the flood,
and this is the world as it is now.
The waters and the islands.

Before we were concerned by wars and plagues and famines,
Commonplace horrors of our own making and scale,
We achieved things on the edge of our own comprehension.
We flew to the stars, and grew… Certain.
So we were simply unprepared for that which was outside our
grasp.

In many ways we are lucky we even survived at all.

Now, no one knows how to make sense of anything.
So they only make sense of it for their own little bit of water,
and of their own little bit of land.

As for why it happened? What caused it? Knowing that does not
help us now. It can't be unbroken, so we have to learn to live with
the pieces.'

The Captain returns to her work,
The people around you scatter,
You are left alone on the deck again.

VOLUME 4: ISLANDS.

Pylons.

Sailing at some distance, the bitter smell of something burnt, plastic maybe metal, comes on the air. Then, old electrical items that may be still functional on your ship, radios and phones, anything with a speaker, begin to pick up signals. A static crackle without a single source has come aboard, and it is wandering your ship like a poltergeist. Then you see the island in the distance, black and silver needles reaching up. They call it the pin cushion.

As you close-in there is a feeling that everything is vibrating. The air tastes different, sour and metallic, as if you had licked a silver lime, and then the hum begins. The hum is in everything. The sea seems to have a softer surface, a haze of tiny particles at the surface, a dancing mist. Even clouds in the sky are blurred around the edges. The sails of your ship, the ropes, even your clothes feel charged with static.

Within a few hundred meters of the island the dead fish begin to flow past the hull, the water carries a latent charge, and your boat picks up static. You would be wise not to handle any metal fittings you may have, or risk being on the end of any number of unexpected shocks.

Once near enough to the island you can make out its central spire among the needles. It is called The Spike, but it is wire-tangled, and uneven – There are rusted dishes, and garden rake antennae, cables weaving through the infrastructure, resting on aerials. It is a voodoo doll into which needles have been stuck, but the flesh of the doll has gone and only its bones remain. It is a tree hollowed out by lightning strikes.

The noise is immense, a throbbing, insistent unrelenting chorus. Every note is being played at once, different shades of static, rhythms buried deep, overlapping and enmeshed. The inhabitants are deaf, due to long exposure, and prone to getting struck by lightning strikes drawn by the needles, which consist of many makeshift aerials and transmitters erected into the sky. The locals carry scars, and strange purple and blue rootlike striations across their skin as reminders of a sharp kiss from the sky.

On arrival you must wait in line with the others who have come, and there are many, standing in line, all wearing ear defenders of some sort, or ear plugs in, and hands pressed to the sides of their head. Locals walk up and down the line trading the waxen earplugs for food, much of which has been brought in advance in expectation.

The line is silent, partially as the sound is too great, and talking to each other would require bellowing into each other's ears, but more so because no one wishes to speak. Everyone is absorbed in an internal conversation, everyone is practicing their lines.

Arrivals are drawn to a courtyard beneath the spike, and there two options are presented; a blackboard, or a booth. Before selection, a payment is made, some form of goods. Then they will choose and walk to waiting attendants.

At the blackboard, they are handed chalk, they write a message, after any discussion needed for the transcription of letters, it is tapped into a morse code receiver, and is sent, the board wiped clean. At the booth, a microphone waits, always live, you step within and whilst briefly barricaded inside against the noise by heavy cloths, you say what is needed, till the curtain is pulled back and light reenters. The result seems always to be the same, a kind of baffled emptiness, the question spent and sent, they walk away, guided by others to their boats.

The island is a prayer channel, the machinery of the island exists solely to send messages, as far and as wide as possible, to the sky, and into the ground. To which gods they do not discriminate, any that might listen. The point is this, the blackboard allows for a precise message to be sent, but it is made publicly to all those waiting. The booth allows a private message, but one that may not be heard accurately amongst the cacophony of other voices.

The words on the board are all effectively the same, questions in only two directions: why did something happen, or will something happen. Or confession seeking forgiveness or acknowledgement. Neither of which is given by those around to witness, too concerned with their own messages to care.

The departing ships and boats often leave in the same direction. Leading away from the island are wires on wooden posts, leaning, sinking, rotting, astray over the shallow water. Another island beckons many who have left a message, and so a caravan departs in hope of a response. Those who neither need or expect it, go their own way.

Summit.

No one lives permanently on the island, but one way or another, almost everyone is here. A few scattered and temporary tents are pinned to manageable surfaces.

It was once one of the tallest mountains in the world. It breaches the surface of the ocean like the body of a gigantic black whale, barnacle encrusted, a glistening balletic mass of fat and muscle, detonating the sea into fragments in all directions from itself, reaching some hundreds of feet into the air, but never crashing down; a crash suspended in time. But it is now merely the peak of a shark's fin, not the tens of thousands of feet it once commanded to survey the world around it, mere hundreds.

Submerged beneath the water are names, and names, and names. The names of people carved into the surface of the mountain by those who needed them, loved them, lost them. The mountain is a monument, a headstone to take the burden of a million names and more.

There are also images at rare points, simple carved images of lost things and places; And lines. Horizontal lines marked in the stone, some which might be misread as underlining the names, some are exactly that. But there are other lines, some dated, some numbered, but the most revealing are those that come with inscriptions, 'two months nothing then this in one day', 'no countries', 'there are fish and birds again', 'about a year of steady rise', 'survivors', 'boats and islands'. The mountain has also been used to chart the progress of the water's rise and fragments of the human narrative. It is an inconsistent timeline of immeasurable events, it is a history.

Above the current waterline, where for now the waters have ceased to rise, a strange collection of carvings begin, there still remain names such Imogen, and Isaac, Adam, and Gillian, but littered amongst them are the names of places and objects from the past: Pyramid, Park, Train, England. But these are not direct memorials, these too are names, parents have carved their own names, and the names of their children, but the names of the living are drawn from the lost icons of the past. Out there in the world 'Fairground' is fishing in clear waters, 'Laptop' is tying off a rope, 'Haybale' is looking at the horizon.

Above the waterline, the high point is an anchor of current culture and life. It is a record of names and where names come from, of what was lost, what was valued, and how it has been transformed. Into marks, into names, into people. Unseen beneath, the mountain of the dead supports them.

Boats.

The old cruise-liners, oil tankers, and container ships are at the centre, a great central mass of steel lashed together with rope and chain, buffered with row upon row of rubber tyres. Around these, acting as a corden ring of fire, are a range of military craft. Aircraft carriers, battle-ships, cruisers and destroyers.

Ships are moved to create great canals for smaller boats to move among the mass. Canalboats scalped of their canopies are the foundation of many of the pathways and borders that canal boats meander through, people hop from boat to boat. The boats that people live in now have picket fences topped with broken glass.

The water is rank with human sewage, spilled oil, and flotsam and jetsam. With the size of the island's population the waste far outreaches its edge. As such no one swims, and children would have to be taken far out to sea to learn, and this is not permitted. Mortality is highest from infection from slipping into the water. People 'drown' with great frequency, but this is a euphemism for murder, with bodies weighted and slipped between hulls never to be seen again.

The island would appear prosperous, for it is constantly busy, but it is constantly hungry and cannibalising itself.

The different ships serve all manner of different functions, but there is no prison ship. This seems strange for such a large gathering of people, but there is a simple reason, there is no imprisonment as a punishment in the laws of the island.

Incarceration simply takes up too much by way of resource, and so when criminal acts occur and culprits are caught, system of punishment is by servitude. The island's ships are maintained by its criminal population. This is set out as a service to all, but the central ships have long since wielded the power and influence, so that the type of work and the duration is controlled by them.

Those deemed of little value, are given dangerous work of cleaning and repairing the hulls of ships. Crimes committed by children and women, have a habit of resulting in long periods of domestic service to those in the central hub, and so on... Those who were the sailors and citizens become the workers, the workers become the slaves. The laws of the island are many, and the enforcers hold a privileged but despised position.

While many had flocked to the mass of boats in the early days, now for many escape is the dream. The island draws in its population as quickly as it tries to leave, life rafts are built to escape, at the rate that small boats arrive.

Calm.

No wind.

No swell.

No islands.

You imagine the sea becomes a mirror of the sky.

Two blue infinities.

You sit on the deck, unmoving,
and listen for anything:
gulls, sails, time.

None come.

The Captain's voice feels disembodied, as if it floats through the
ship. If you did not hear her moving around the ship. You would
think she wasn't there.

After a while, you forget what movement felt like.

You begin to wonder if you've stopped existing too.

Ash.

Here under perpetual falling ash and a blacked landscape are a happy and hopeful people. They must daily navigate rivers of lava, and at night be mindful of any new flows spilling over from the mouth. Frequently there are small earthquakes and minor eruptions, their homes can topple, they can be burned or maimed and even killed by falling magma. As they move around the island they must be careful where they tread in case there is a burning chamber beneath them, and the crust of the caldera too thin to hold their weight. There is no natural shelter on the island, no source of freshwater. All sustenance is drawn from the sea, water from the sky. They are a happy people.

As they live, they sing songs about the blackened ground, and compose poems and stories involving lava flows making their way to the sea, all as metaphors for the inevitability that all will be good in the future. They use falling ash to make drawings, and for dyes, and makeup.

They would appear to be religious, and you would be forgiven for imagining they worship the active volcano they reside on. But their culture gives no reference to any god at all or space of worship, there is none of the common personification of a natural phenomena; an angry fire god, a god with a gift of fire for example. Their stories do not involve end time prophecies of the volcano erupting and destroying the island.

Instead they tell stories of the island expanding and growing till its exhaustion from labour leads to a paradisiacal future of sleep. The stories are not myths, they are projections of what they see everyday, their world expands moment by moment before their eyes. Each morning there is a drum beat and singing. There are songs about magma, celebrations for plant-life, about migration birds finding the island, about the fertility of the volcanic earth.

The islanders wake, and take up their labours, in various areas around the island, to the beat of the drum, they crush rocks. Heavy wooden timbers, lifted and dropped, in time to the beat, making the beat... For boulders, the largest hammers, the slowest rhythm... From there to smaller rocks, a mid tempo, and between those beats stamping away, are platformed wooden clogs of a kind, bound to the feet and crushing to dust what is left... This grinding of the smallest of rocks is less a drumming and more a dance. The swift stamping, twists and twirls, designed to grind the smallest particles. The whole endeavour would seem ceremonial, with the music, song and dances seemingly like courtship displays of physical stamina, and health; Perhaps they will eventually become this, but not yet. The process is designed to create soil, at an accelerated rate, and from this to replant and grow generous crops.

There is nothing here to draw larger numbers of inhabitants. The transformation of the island is imperceptible and generations away. This slowness makes it safe. They are not afraid of the volcano erupting violently, they accept this as inevitable. If it does so, then it only proves there is yet more life and land to come.

Long ago, people dreamt of reaching the stars and terraforming new worlds, here the new world is being formed, by the world itself.

'Old Fires burn,
Blue Oceans turn,
Black earth it grows,
And Green it goes,
The land it works, and so shall we.

Once land it overcomes the sea,
We sleep, we'll dream, we join the stream.'

Containers.

Each one is the expression of its owner. Beauty is stacked on beauty. The island is a wonder at a distance, and disappoints in no way as one nears. Hundreds of brightly coloured metal cargo containers piled high in irregular pyramids, all centred around a central mass.

It resembles its own technicolour mountain range, festooned with ropes and climbing ladders, suspended pathways and bridges. The containers themselves are vivid colours, every colour and shade, no one colour near another. The containers facing west and east bleach in the sun. The colour palette of the whole island is stitched together with greens – seaweeds darkly mass over the lowest level soon replaced by soft dense mosses and scaly lichens. These give way to ivy, creepers, and climbing flowers that exploit any crevasse or gap or untended section.

Above which the island forms into uneven patches and layers of meadow or woodland copse. These grow on top of the containers. Thin topsoil laid down by inhabitants and protected, and allowing roots into or around their containers.

Inside each container a different family builds a world. The containers are dark, and light is given access in two ways; through small holes tunnelled from the outside, to provide spotlights on certain areas; and the double doors of the container which are thrown open on warm days. The interiors are cramped but well organised, and kept meticulously clean. They must be for fear of vermin. Between each container, in the narrow spaces formed by accident, closed off by root networks, filled up with detritus, parallel ecologies have established themselves. Worms, beetles, and grubs endeavour to turn the world to compost around them. Ants build mycological farms and cities of negative space one tunnel after another. Then in larger tunnels the rats create their runs to traverse the whole island. The rats are loathed, for fear of disease and their consumption of food stores.

The islanders have combatted this problem with the introduction of cats. The island is overrun with them, none belong to a particular container or family, but clearly bonds have been established. The cats live from hunting the rodent population, but are groomed and sheltered by the islanders. When doors are opened in the mornings, it's not uncommon for a feline outpouring to occur. In the afternoons, the upper edges of containers are populated by the community of cats, whiskers fluttering in the breeze, fur warmed by the sun. The children of the islanders think the cats built the island, and play hunting games of Cat and Rat frequently switching roles. But no one really wants to be a Rat.

Seaweed.

The garden of the new world is green and gold and blue. Twin blue hemispheres of sky and sea, bisected by a line of silken fronds of treasure, held tight to reflect the sun. Seaweed, one of the first plants, one of the first foods, has become the last and most abundant. The first plant is the last plant.

The seaweed is tended both above and below the horizon. Gardeners paddle in an ungainly fashion on the surface defying the sea with netted shoes that carry their weight. They scare off birds, pick flotsam and jetsam from the surface, clean waste that floats in on the tide. Wide brimmed hats so large as to shade their entire bodies all day long.

Below they free-dive, weighted with rocks against their legs. Stores of air are dropped to different levels, upturned waxed baskets, for the divers to pause in as they ascend and descend. These are set each morning, and also provide respite or shelter from heavy seas and storms. Through a system of weights and pulleys they can be raised to the surface, take on new air and dropped again for prolonged submersion.

The surface is where the gardeners take shelter and dry themselves. Their homes are not islands as such, but rather boats of a sort. Floating in the seaweed, or resting on the rocks just below the surface, not designed to sail anywhere. They live in wide circular coracles, giant bowls the size of houses, each holding several families. The bowls are panel beaten and sturdy things, rusted, barnacled, and seaweed strewn themselves. Each one tilts at some slight angle, and with strong waves or tides rotates and rolls, like poorly made crockery on a table.

Each bowl is topped with a lid to provide shade and keep out the rain. These discs are propped up with sticks. As bowls move like slow motion spinning tops, small hands appear and adjust the angle removing and replacing the supports one by one. Occasionally a lid will slam shut by accident, projecting a sharp resonant boom across the sea. At other times, when there is a threat, or incoming heavy seas, nearby ships can receive a prior warning by harkening the flurry of echoing bowls snapping shut.

Once in a while, a bowl may be dislodged from the mass of seaweed, and drift in the oceans like a coconut, till the tide takes it to the shore of some other island. Rarer still one comes across an emptied bowl, adrift, and pried open by pirates, the insides scoured and pillaged, like a bird might consume a Whelk. The lid torn and open like an old tin can.

Field.

Barbed wire is honest. It states its aim and methodology with indifferent clarity. Stay away, I will cut you. And even though it is rarely used on the island, for every boundary drawn, by every inhabitant of the island, the sentiment remains the same.

Some inhabitants build walls of old imported stone to give the appearance of a long standing border – This historic line should not be crossed. Others use picket fences with echoes of long since lost polite village cottages and colonial legacies – We've made such improvements here, please take care. A few resort to hedgerows threaded with brambles. A kind of high status version of barbed wire that conceals its armory within a cloak of managed nature. The most deliberately unpleasant inhabitants plant trees at their boundaries. This is deemed aggressive, as the roots go underground and across borders, drinking water from a neighbour's land, The branches go up over and across, dropping leaves. One cannot stop a tree from being a tree. Disputes over trees, more than any other boundary, cause fatalities.

For all the raising of boundaries, the inhabitants do their best to whittle away at them; Walls are deconstructed, stone by stone; Trees trimmed; fence posts wobbled in the ground to loosen them in advance of strong winds.

The island is divided into hundreds of tiny rectangular strips. Each strip of land is fertile, and the islanders cling to it with ferocity, as for some time they have been self-sufficient. The island is organised around a committee with many members. There are many meetings and many arguments. Boundaries are contested, disputes over water, managed. Each islanders hates their neighbour. Before our arrival, the island was an open field.

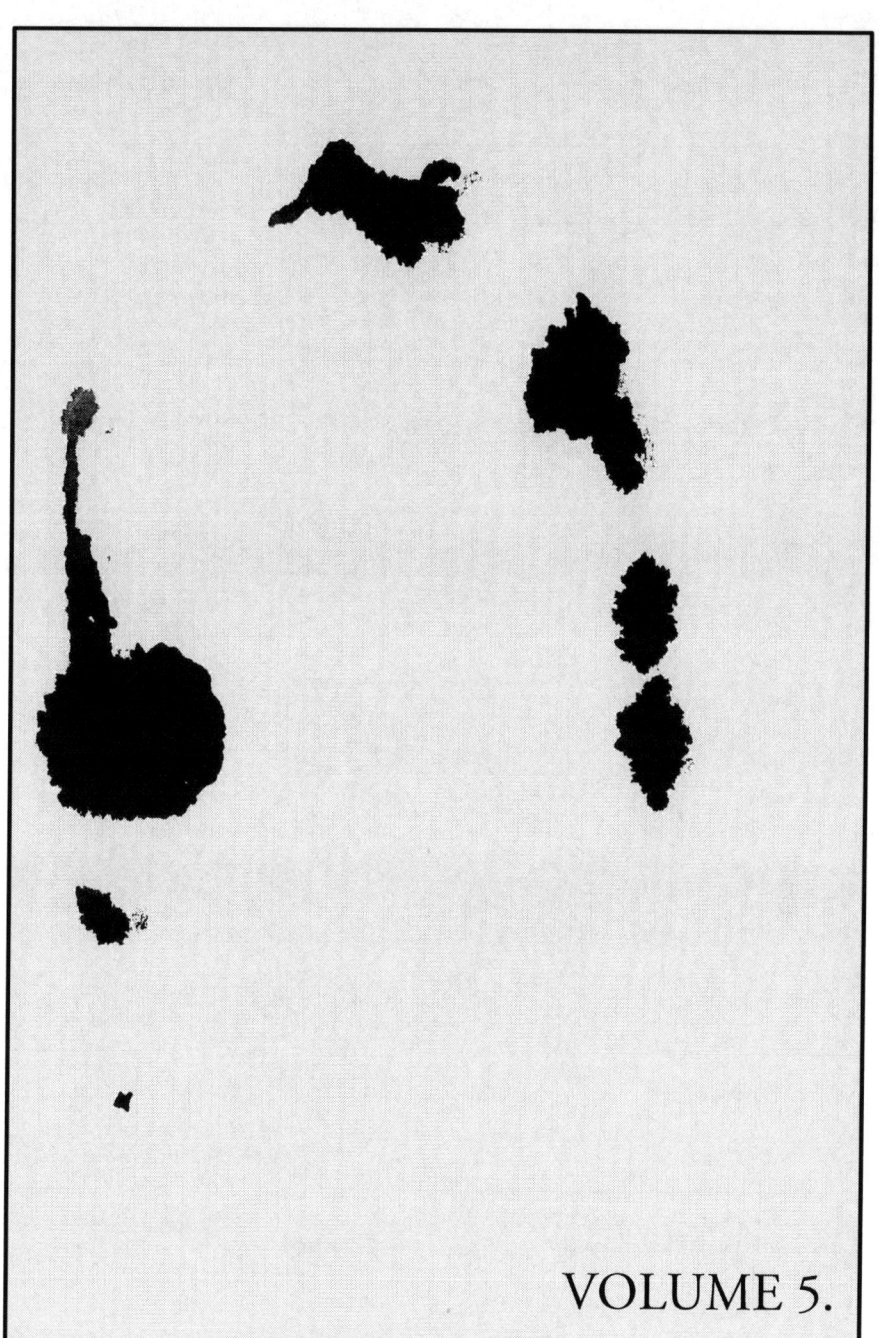

VOLUME 5.

Seeds.

The ship makes its stops,
It docks with other ships,
It makes port.

It meets with other ships,
Others are invited on board,
Listening to the accounts of islands visited,
They write these down.

At islands, children and adults alike,
Come just to hear these tales,
While business is conducted.

At one island the smallest parcels of seeds are brought aboard,
These are handed over at a very specific sets of islands,
Each one with fertile ground,
Replanting,
Reseeding.

Messages are passed from island to island – through the ship.

Other ships come alongside for navigation,
Not to find the islands,
But to find the currents followed,
Deadwaters,
To relocate the wandering stars,
To name persistent and occasional winds.

On board this ship, aboard all the ships that sail,
Worlds are being made between the islands.

The whispers from islanders about the ship and Captain continue. You begin to piece together that the Captain is delivering messages from one place to another, your maps are being recounted to cartographers, information about the inhabitants of certain islands and the movements of certain ships is gathered, never directly, but indirectly.

On many islands you begin to notice a pattern; a visit, trade and discussions, and departure. Then only a few hours after leaving, a second landing, a brief excursion from the boat, before returning.

You do not know what the Captain does on these second visits. You ask the Captain, all you get is:

'We plant questions.'
'We witness until witnessing becomes a kind of harm.'
'We try to deliver another future.'

VOLUME 5: ISLANDS.

Park.

The wonders of the ancient world are lost under the oceans. The Egyptian Pyramids are green, festooned with seaweed. Stonehenge is lost in silt. So there must be new ancient wonders, now from the ruins of the modern world, still ruined, redundant of prior purpose, but still revered. Sites that seem as if they were made by giants or gods.

They are marked by a sense of permanence. That their construction was made for something greater than people, and that as time crumbled or shattered other places – the passage of people through these places simply smoothed their roughness, polished them, hardened and compacted them, to make them monumental.

When modern people touched the ancient wonders, they knew those walls were not just shaped by those that made and lived with them, but by every person since. All those who had sought out their mystery. Tens of Thousands of fingertips and palms brushing stone to near glass finish, a layered varnish of the oil in our skin that only obscured the true surface underneath.

And so the walls inside an ancient pyramid's tomb, and the walls inside this island, share this same quality. For the ceilings, walls and floors are rendered and finished by human touch. And as the uses of ancient wonders fall into mystery and are reconstructed as myth. The name of this island is also divided and rearranged, into four distinct words, to speak to its new status of an ancient wonder. Air Park Car Port.

One docks at the ports freshly constructed from scavenged materials, surrounding the layered stack on concrete perched on the hill, the multi-story carpark. It must have been an unremarkable blight on whatever airport it once belonged to, but now with all the many smaller buildings surrounding it washed and cleared away, it is a charcoal diamond, a primal shape that feels as if it has existed long before humans, a rare geological fluke, that we've recalled though millennia and instinctively recalled. Older than all the wonders, something from when the earth was hot and molten.

It is empty. All the cars have been removed, and now form a protective wall around it, doubling as living spaces and the foundations for new constructions, and the building blocks of buildings themselves that serve the island's inhabitants. These are full of people and noise. They trade from cars, they sleep in cars, they are born and die in cars. The car park itself has been forbidden as a site for sustained habitation. But it is not empty of life.

At Air Park Car Port hundreds come to walk, to sleep, to sing. Level by level a single simple human activity fills the space, among the supporting pillars, and on the intersecting coiling ramps. On one level crowds purposefully walk from edge to edge, or stroll in circles, individuals or pairs meander here and there. Above, the floors are strewn with layered blankets and prone figures collectively at different stages of sleep. Bodies deep in sleep buried and weighted under insulating layers, and others drifting dreaming; rolling or lifting limbs that flop back to slowly breathing torsos when gravity becomes too much. These bodies are lulled by the vibrations in the floor from the level below, and lullabied by the sounds from above. One level up, the chorus sings, the softest song. Hundreds sit or stand, but do not move bar breathing and ushering from their throats close harmonies. No words, just long held outward breaths adrift through vocal cords vibrating sending waves into the empty space which fills with every other voice, and every echo from the walls. The song does not begin or end, it rises, falls, and swells and fades, it follows the sea the day, the weather, seasons and the moon. It pours out from Air Park Car Port, and is heard for miles around.

At the highest level the island has imported earth from somewhere, to produce a wildflower meadow, leading to a gentle slope, a modest hill topped with a copse of trees. An orchard. Here they grow apples, a staple food, and also good for making cider. With the orchard comes a need to ensure pollination, and so the islanders also keep bees. The hives dotted around the meadow. So from the orchard comes apples, wood, honey, cider, and purified alcohol. Above the orchard, the sky – and from its open sides the sky, the sea and the horizon.

We used to fly, we remember the planes, we know they would glide into land, or rise to leave trails in the sky. We would travel to this place in cars, and leave them waiting. Then we would fly, we could go anywhere in the world. Imagine that. The runways are washed away now. So now people sit on the exposed edges of Air Park Car Port and wait, staring up and out from the wonder, for the mechanical ghosts of the past, having walked among the deserted resting place of cars. Hoping for a glimpse of a haunted sky.

Birds.

It first appears as an optical illusion – a disturbance of light, a shimmering mass, heat waves in the air, debris on the water – as if there were no island after all. Yet there is a foundation, a substantial rocky plateau, but it is rarely accessible, and an indistinct shape rises above it, the shifting outline of an island. It is a colossal frenzy of birds. Every species one can imagine.

The murmuration takes many forms. It can tower above the island in a spindle, shrink into a low squat swirling sphere, or spread out to an uneven mass that contains shapes and weird dynamics within its loose boundaries. There are appearances of oyster mushrooms, petal edges, clouds and angular formations – Strings, Densities, planes and sound waves – Scatterings, turns, accelerations and mergers.

As you watch, everything blends, each atomised speck of life is a hazy blur. But look for long enough and your eyes will receive a puncturing stab of a single bird, wings splayed beak thrust claws curled, all at once. A blush of colours standing out. Even rarer you might grasp in your sight a sequence of wings, or tails, a clutch of birds in union, before they vanish in the flock.

The island can vanish with great rapidity. Mass landings occur in silence as if conducted, following a downward hushing gesture, fingers splayed. The flock will rest, chattering and squawking. For moments, minutes, every Bird can be seen – every species, size and gender. Crows and Sparrows, Albatross and Owl, chicken, parrot, eagle, dove, vulture, ibis, wren, flamingo. Then before your mind can comprehend the sight, a sudden upward outward bloom, and all are in flight, as if a cue of silent fingers clicked had launched them. Silhouetted flecks, like voids in space and time, moving across the sky.

The island never really settles, the birds are in constant motion, wings, tails, beaks overlapping, movement in every direction, with no fixed point for the eye to rest upon, no measure of depth to gauge, the flock resembles a field of static. All possible colours, leveling to a steady grey. Deep in the static, one cannot help but see patterns, but unlike the hesitant outlines mapped in murmurations, the static makes ghostly masses, solid shapes seen moving behind the avian veil. Some come to view these shapes, to glean meaning. But soon those who come are troubled and depart. The more you look the more you see that the shapes and masses in the flock are not for us, that if there is meaning there, it is for the birds themselves and them alone.

The island is bearable depending upon the time of day. When the birds do rest, on the surface of the water or walking the island, visitors can float alongside them, pick their way through them. But when they launch or land it can be perilous, and sudden drownings and mass attacks have been known. The dawn chorus is deafening, and ships retreat from it.

Then one day they are gone. The flock is migratory, but routes and other resting points have not been discovered.

Heaps of feathers are blown across the ocean, tides are left to strike the island, the rock itself white with calcified waste is washed clean and black, and shortly seaweed limpets and barnacles return, crabs emerge from beak and claw proof crevices.

The island remains untouched for months, till a dark speck on the horizon heralds the return of the flock.

Shadows.

'Do you remember who you were before this voyage?'

You ask the question while seated on the deck, twisting coils of rope by feel, tracing the rough salt-set fibres. Above you, the mainsail flaps against the wind. The smell of tar, wet wool, rusted metal. She doesn't answer immediately. The sound of her boots fades. You wonder if she's walked away.

'Only in the wrong light,' she says at last, voice low. You turn your head toward the sound.

'Then I catch a glimpse,' she continues, 'of a woman I don't recognise. One with dry hands. Fewer knives. Softer thoughts.' She shifts her weight. The deck creaks.

'I lost her on an island with no name. Then again at sea. Then I carved up her remains, and used her for parts.'

You reach out, but stop short of touching her. 'Do you miss her?'

'Sometimes. But she wouldn't survive out here now.' There's silence. The ship tilts. A gull calls, then disappears into the sky.

'And you?' she asks, after a while. 'Do you remember who you were, before I found your ship on fire?'

'No.' you say.
'Then be who you are now,' she replies. 'And we'll keep afloat as long as we can.'

Scaffold.

It is a masterpiece of angles and planes, surfaces and lines. A blank house of cards, frozen mid-collapse, festooned with cobwebs. It is hard to look at in the sunlight. It glows.

It is an island covered in scaffolding, but that barely registers, beneath it ramshackle higgledy-piggledy flat-roofed dwellings cover the ground in its totality. Then before the dwellings and hung upon the scaffolding, are screens. A multitude of sizes, facing the sea in all directions around the island. A shell around the island, made from a range of materials: sail-cloth, plastic, whitewashed driftwood. Blank during the day, quiet, dead… Once the sun has set, the island comes alive – The projectors are turned on.

For everything there used to be in the old world, there is now a screen to replay it, and everything is screened. Any footage from any source is shown without discrimination. All propped up by steel, and nuts and bolts. As if the clothes of a world could be hung on the bones of another, to bring it back to life. Colours are hurled at the screens and people emerge to sit on the rooftops and watch. Travelers have come to marvel at the old world. There is no soundtrack, bar the natural shuffling movement of people and their hushed mutterings. Occasionally the crowds involuntarily provide a score, making noises to accompany what is seen – which among the cross legged masses builds-up and makes a vague mockery of the sounds of the past. A past which few, if any, would remember.

Despite this, some to pretend to remember the old world. No one believes them, and perhaps they are not trying to convince anyone but themselves – maybe not even that, maybe they feign recognition as an act of faith, if it can be remembered, it was real.

They sit and stare at the screens and murmur to themselves 'yes, that's where I lived', 'yes, I owned one of those', 'yes it happened', 'yes, that's what it was like'… when it was nothing of the sort. They believe the world was a series of graspable objects, single events, and unchanging places. When the old world was just like the new one, an ongoing collision of landslides.

Most visitors will leave despondent, coming down, from the high of spectacle back into the dulled wreckage of the world. But others will be mesmerised, fixed at the screens, and so people will starve to death, gawping. Their mouths open at the screen, open-wide in hunger, with nothing to eat but light. Eventually, dislocated jaws will sweep loose from rotting corpses or skeletons. Amongst the remains you notice the teeth, the lower halves of expressions of wonder dropped from the top, as if an invisible cut had been made when awestruck.

Dead.

The dead now will not leave us, they are a continent adrift.

And how will people know if they are dead? And how will people know if they are alive? For as the moon drives the tides, the waves give breath to the dead, it makes them shift uneasy.

The gnawing tug of a feeding shark beneath the surface will make the dead turn over. Bloating bodies will sit up briefly in memorial to themselves. A strong wind will pick up limbs and make them gesture, and a sea swell forms a parade of the dead, a tumbling wall, our ancestors falling.

The island of the dead is colourful, clothed as it is in every fashion of the world, and rainbow blue with the shine of flies, and hues of rot. As bodies fall apart new colours bloom, and every scrap of clothing lashed and tangled. The clothes that hold us warm in life, are the ropes that hold the island tight.

The living who reside on the island are indistinguishable from the dead at a distance. No one stands on the island of the dead, they crawl from torso to torso, grasping from spine to spine as handholds. They rest upon the leathered faces of those who dried out in the sun, and survive among fresh pickings, and the animals that come to feed. At the fringes, sodden hands reach out as if to gently play, idly dipping fingers in the water, while other hands work just a softly, but with purpose, pulling in new bodies, tying knots.

The island of the dead hums, hymns, and buzzes and sighs. It sings a song – The island teems with life. Crabs and fish and birds and flies will pick and peck, till bone shows through… and that same flash of white tells of a body bound to sink, bone by bone to the bed below, leaving not a heap, but a broken line of ready-bleached false coral behind the island's tidal drift above. The trail of slaughterhouse breadcrumbs below, is also joined by a caravan of carrion feeders, shambling in the dark.

The dead fall from the skies above to nourish them, they follow.

Task.

The sacks she carries are not provision but legacy. She scatters them where no harvest waits, among ruins where no hand will gather.

'These are not gifts for men,' she tells you. 'They are futures for the ground, for the gulls, for the silence that will follow us.'

While she casts seed into broken soil, she sets you to remember.

'Hold it in the atlas of your mind,' she says. 'Every coast, every folly, every fire. Not for return, but so the world is known to have been.'

The work is doubled: seed in the soil, islands in memory. Both for a time that will not include you.

You ask what she wants from you — beyond remembering all these islands. Why not do it herself, or write them down?

She ties something off, adjusts a pulley, and finally says:

'I cannot be what you are going to become, no more than you can become me.'

You do not ask again.

But you lie awake longer that night, trying to imagine what an atlas in your mind might do to you.

Wall.

The wall is incredibly old. Its origins have sunk into myth. It covers thousands of miles, and is the largest structure to survive intact above the water. It runs a ragged course roughly east to west and was said to mark the border of a country. Large portions are beneath the water, but they now act as the foundations of extensions to the wall, and bridges built since the oceans rose. Its design appears as one of fortification, yellow stone with castellation on the edge and turreted forts along the way. Now it defends nothing, it borders nowhere. It is its own island, and a series of towns and villages run along it. Wooden buildings are built on balconies on either side. Some reach over the wall to create short tunnels. But no building spreads out too far from the wall, not blocks the main thoroughfare. They build alongside and up, as the path atop the wall now defines its purpose.

The wall is the great promenade of the world. Countless people travel from across oceans to be able to walk and make progress by foot across a landscape. The wall walkers generally keep to the left, but there are more walkers east to west to keep the morning sun at their back. And the way is never obstructed, with vendors and businesses and houses set back from the path. Those form the towns and villages, the largest being the five main distance markers which are named prosaically East End, West End, East and West Quarter, and Half (Which is officially titled Half-Way, but no one calls it that).

East End is considered the starting point of those who wish to undertake the walking pilgrimage, with West End as the definitive destination. As such those cities take different shapes. West End is perhaps the exception to the rule; a circular city, that spreads out around the wall, and its final turret on an endless maze of floating pontoons. Pilgrims queuing on the pathway to have their moment of reaching the end. Sometimes staying for weeks, before a final wait in line to do so.

East end is a narrow city, but one that keeps expanding back eastwards, building more wall to accommodate the numbers of people who wish to start. The wall at east end is the newest, straightest, and longest straight section of the wall itself. The market for outward provisions maintains this growth.

The quarter towns and the city of Half are where people take extended rests, or quit or postpone their walk for a later return. Those are seen as honorable points to stop. Many bloodied feet, and crawling hobbling figures can be seen struggling to these points to make a proper stop if injury or misfortune has been encountered.

Violence along the route is rare. Theft is uncommon, when it does occur it is propelled by a lack of preparation. Exhaustion and accident, the weather and storms can throw people from the wall, high tides sending unexpected waves over the battlements. In more neglected areas of the wall is not maintained, one can simply trip, fall, and twist or break a limb. Some hundred miles from a village, this can be fatal even with assistance.

Those that walk the wall define it. A steady stream of travellers making their way from one end to another. The wall is maintained to keep the way open for them, not as habitation, border, or defences. Nightly teams of builders emerge, paid for by the cities to walk a portion of the wall and check for erosion in the mortar, a new pebble caught between the edges, a crack caused by a hard morning frost, the slightest tilt of subsidence in a stone. Some establishments take territorial care of their section of the way, washing it, dusting, even polishing it. In one village a rug festival is held, with hundreds of woven masterpieces laid out for walkers to tread barefoot upon. In another during late summers, water is pumped onto the surface of the wall to make a cooling ankle deep lake for walkers to wade in. Another village marks a winter festival by lining the way after sunset with great burning pyres, creating a half mile furnace, which while warming to begin with, is a relief to escape from at the end in the cold and dark of the night.

Castle.

They have a castle, outside the bounds of which is land enough to grow crops and domesticate animals. They have accepted or they perform an idea of a feudal system, a lord and his family preside over the community. They have servants, courtiers, even a jester. But the islanders are aware of this as a fiction. They can, as does everyone else, remember systems of governance and economics that succeeded. But there is a thought that pervades the island, one that humanity or at least the project of humanity being able to civilise and progress has failed, and has now been rendered unobtainable. So now they tell themselves that they need a strong leader, that corruption is inevitable, that power flows through the hands of men. They tell themselves that this is natural, and that they are in fact closer to God this way.

The castle itself, on closer inspection reveals clues to its own past, long after it was built and used, it was partially destroyed in a war, after that it was abandoned, later still it was rebuilt and restored by modern owners, heating systems plumbed in, drainage installed, wiring running behind skirting boards. Later still the castle was gifted by these owners to the country, whence it became a museum and tourist attraction, and so as a result, the storage spaces of the castle still contain faded information boards about the history of the site, whose accuracies are ignored, and box upon box of useless merchandise. Finally, when the space had lost all sense of value, it became a 'Business hub', improvements and additions were made. That mostly involved stripping out every space of domesticity and tourism and heritage to maximise the space for utility and functionality.

Afterwards, everything was put in reverse, in all the main spaces, were scavenged for raw materials, carpeting lifted, furniture burnt, writing pulled from the walls, plumbing and pipes melted down. In a matter of weeks the building was reduced to a state of skeletal remains not seen since its construction.

This is where they live, in a position of retreat, clinging to a near fictional idea of the past, in a relic made habitable by its future, the very one they say gave them nothing.

VOLUME 6.

Pioneer.

The Captain has joined you in the dark.
Today though she pulls off her gloves,
Unwraps the bandages from her hands,
And asks 'After years at sea what am I now?'

'Barnacle Knuckles,
Starfish suckle fingertips and palm.
Kelp-veined and Sharktooth nailed,
Muscle fish-flesh.
Deeper still scrimshaw,
Uncarving itself to Whalebone.
Is my blood my own or squid ink?
No break of skin, no lumps or gouges.
Each change curated, situated,
To sustain the shape and surface,
Of my original self.
Each change adds new patterns,
As if there were tattoos beneath the skin,
Welcome nuances, additions,
To what was there before.
I am accumulating the world,
Rearranged cell by cell,
No longer closed to it.'

She tells you that the descriptions she gives of islands,
Are charting the topography of the world,
But the world itself is drawing a second map,
One of new phenomena and flesh,
Charted within her own.

VOLUME 6: ISLANDS.

Themepark.

The pretty lights and colours and screams can be seen and heard from far away. A crimson hue fills the night sky, and at the level of the horizon the sparklingly yellow golden lights are twirling and flashing. The lights rise from the sea up into the air as the island rests on a 45 degree angle protruding toward the sky.

Boats come from far away every day to arrive at sunset to see the spectacle of the fun-fair, to smell the burnt sugar sweetness of candy floss and caramel dipped apples in the air, blended with the oil and grease of the machines. They come for the gaudy displays painted onto the facades and to walk, and be seen by other pleasure seekers – desiring eyes wide open and inviting as they pass each other. They come for the rides themselves, to place themselves in machines that will hurl their bodies at speed in circles, along tracks, into the sky to plummet, into mutual collision, again and again to old music pushed through speakers at their limit. They ride the machines screaming with joy and terror mingled, adrenaline thrills matched with jolts and bruises, nausea and delirium. They stumble from a ride gasping, and stumble to another through the mud, tokens exchanged for entry. With each ride the mud is scrapped from boots, and no one mentions it…

That the foundations are not secure. That cables cold and thick are taut and latched to each and every ride, that anchors have been driven in the ground, that winches pull the rides back every morning up the hill, because the island, the Themepark, is slowly sliding into the sea. No one looks downhill at the saltwater swamp, where carousel horses are slowly drowning, their fixed racing-effort faces now pained and desperate grimaces against the mud and crusted salt around their necks. A big wheel part sunk leaves sad immobile carriages with meagre views like an eye half closed. Further down where the waves lap harmlessly against clots of seaweed, fading signage and broken lightbulbs can be seen through the tidal murk. Extending out into the waters the ditched remains of distractions past are rusting.

Yet every night the revellers return, and ride the rollercoaster ever closer to the sea, each night the turn dips them closer to the horizon and oblivion, and while the Themepark slips some inches more than they can pull it back, they still collect prizes of no value, plastic toys and neon coloured bears, awarded for playing games requiring no skill. They play because they cannot stop the island's descent, so they will use up every resource it has, till it has gone.

Conifers.

A shock of lush dark green erupting from the horizon, capped with a dusting of Snow. It never really thickens as the winds are too strong, the snow is always a powder, the trees always in motion, and the fronds of the conifers too soft and pliant to carry weight. So the island appears to materialise from the white sky above, fading into the dense copse below before a jagged line of hard white cuts the trees off before their trucks are revealed. The collar of white above the sea is Bone. The island is a Boneyard.

It is one of many islands called the boneyards. The remains of every land borne creature piled high, washed clean, scraped white by the sun, on the rocky promontories or hung from trees on the east and westward sides of the isle. The marrow inside dried and broken inside.

There are other Boneyard islands, but none with the cultural and manufacturing reputation of The Conifers. The island is famed for its skills and craft in ivory or any other bone production, the quality of its broth made from marrow, and the music of the island.

The gift of the island is its healthy stock of conifers, rich in sap, fed by a freshwater stream from the rock. The trees produce the sap all year round and the sap is in turn used to create a resin or glue. This in itself is traded as a valuable commodity

In amongst the trees an architectural marvel awaits, pathways through the forest are neatly tessellated ribs giving way to clearings that are more akin to plazas with flat shoulder blades

Among the trees and around the trunks themselves are spherical shelters which are constructed in a spiraling weave resembling a paper wasps nest, but made from cut and shaped bone fragments aligned mosaic like with baroque adornments of tooth and tusk, knuckle or joint, and curving frames of spinal column for doors and windows.

In these houses, fresh bone is worked to various ends as the sap is drawn and refined directly from the tree. Every tree of maturity will have one or a number of hollow bones struck into the trunk to create a tap from which the sap can flow.

The island is fed by the bones it works on, as in order to supply the island, fresh bones arrive daily and in the preparation process, marrow is extracted and cooked to produce a salted and long lasting Marrow Broth, of great nutritional value. It too is flavoured with sap to add a slight sweetness.

The combination of resin and bone allows for various other products to be made. Structures of any shape and size can theoretically be realised. The island is famous for its ornamentation to ships, the construction of shelters, and handheld tools, weaponry and armour. The island is strongly defended by a core guard of warriors who wield bladed cudgels made from the thigh bones of previous intruders, the armour from their shoulder blades.

Music also forms an unlikely central aspect of the island's culture, bones are hollowed, carved and combined to form a variety of musical instruments. Wind instruments are the primary outcome, but skin and ligature can also be located and cured to provide percussive surfaces and strings. As such in addition to a variety of flute style instruments, drum, violins and even a crude piano have been made. Many residents are proud of their skill in creation, and as such there is an equal pride in the mastery in the composition and performance of music.

Of course it is well known, but less remarked upon, that the supply of bones to the island is based on a regular delivery of human corpses, from various locations. The bone broth of the island is mostly human marrow, the soft notes of music played through the limbs of descendants.

Below.

On the surface of the ocean is nothing, the slick ripples reflecting the sky, but looking inward nothing still, the layered silt and particles thickening to obscure a downward view.

But if one were able to see through the murk, past the algae, seaweed, and fish and microorganisms swarming, underneath the weight of the waters, are the ruined cities of the modern world, deeper still the ruined cities of the ancient word, below them, nothing but the dark, and the grey wastes, occasionally scattered with waste from every era of humanity, whatever fell from any boat, from early fishing spear to shipwreck.

Then at certain points the plains give way to where the continental plates meet and ridges build. Here the thermal vents rise. Crustacean forms latched on, dipping hardened claws into superheated plumes.

Then nothing again until the abyss to the final depths. There the last life forms hover, miniscule, cellular, barely life.

Finally, below, in the depths beyond the where the crust of the earth had opened many millennia ago, and cooled in millennia since, where there had been molten rock, but now where the water is as black and cold and as compacted as the silt and as the rock, where everything is only mineral, and slow processes creep onto clocks set running when the universe started.

Here – there is a light.

Soundings.

The ship teaches you what the eye has lost.

Halyards tick like clocks. A slack line means lagoon. A rope strained tight announces a headland.

The hull hums a long vowel when the swell lengthens.

You keep no chart in ink — yours is in your hands, in the mast's tremor against your teeth.

The Captain names towers, scaffolds, spires, but you already hear their weight in the rigging.

She nods when you say what is coming, because she knows you read the timbers as she reads the air.

You are not here to measure for return. You are here to remember.

Your soundings are another kind of planting — the map you carry is a seed sown into silence.

When the sea rises over all of it, these patterns may remain, like roots pressed into clay.

Seasons.

Your senses are stripped: no light, no horizon, no breath of wind. The ship is a coffin set adrift. You lie on your bunk and listen to the knots creak.

You try not to sleep.

You try not to remember the island with four seasons at once.

The island is divided cleanly into four.

A perfect cross, marked by walls of hedgerow and wind, by shifts in colour and temperature.

In the northeast, it is spring: earth wet with promise, every branch in bud, bees in their early clumsy flights. In the southeast, summer: heat waves rising off red clay, cracked ground and ripe fruit.

To the southwest, autumn: gold, ochre, and crimson leaves drifting in slow spirals; soft winds and fading light. And in the northwest, winter: bare limbs of trees, snow packed into crevices, the sky thin as glass.

The people here walk in slow spirals, changing direction with the seasons. Some are lost. Others never intend to leave.

Bridges.

An island of 'On-the-way-ness'. Defined precisely by its 'Not-quite-ness' in similarity to other islands. 'The island that isn't the wall', 'The island that isn't the piers'. People call it 'Bridges'. Not even 'The Bridges' or 'Bridge Island'.

A huge red suspension bridge takes centre stage, under which a long silver ribbon of a bridge cuts above the waters. Then cobbling out in every direction a multitude of every other kind of bridge imaginable. Towered, stone, wooden, steel, humpbacked, rope-bridge, Glass and Cantilever. Truss and Beam, cable stayed and Tied Arch. Painted, rusting, rotting, fresh, well maintained and derelict.

 Each bridge arrives at a junction of other bridges. The smallest connecting platform needed to accommodate the join is manufactured. Sometimes a bridge is extended in its own material to meet another, though more often a patchwork of surfaces are thrown together, old planks, thick plastic, chucks of concrete, corrugated metal, wire and string. Each junction feels like some kind of never revealed connective tissue, the stuff that holds the world together that we are never meant to see, on 'Bridges' no one tarries or waits at junctions, it is considered bad luck. The overall effect is that of creating a network, the island resembles a root structure, like the threads of a mould spreading out half-chance half-design. With junctions never lingered at, it is an island of perpetual motion, of people on their way, changing direction, meeting, beginning again.

Habitats are built under the bridges, hanging like hammocks. Thick weathered ropes are slung over the walkways of the bridges and forming their own supportive webs, but also the surface that everyone walks upon. The islanders refer to themselves as 'Trolls' and visitors as 'Goats'. Visitors are encouraged to walk barefoot on the island, while ropes are strong and well maintained, locals would prefer their home not to suddenly fall into the sea if a rope were accidentally damaged by a misplaced boot.

The island has little in the way of produce, so it has become by chance an island of intellectual trade, by way of solutions. Different bridges are associated with different branches of thought, engineering, mathematical, chemical, biological. Trolls emerge onto the walkways each morning to be greeted by Goats who have problems. Trolls will be paid to listen, paid to arrive at solutions, and paid further should the solution work. Sometimes Trolls can be hired in groups, on rare occasions an entire bridge may be devoted to a single problem for a particularly wealthy individual or the representatives of an entire island. The pedestrian and meandering nature of the island in the way supports its function, Trolls may wander up and down their bridge while thinking, rest in thought underneath it, compete or collaborate with neighbours, and even take in alternate perspectives from those on other Bridges. It is well known that the Trolls have designed the mechanisms of some of the great moving islands, their stilts or pulley systems; Formulated the chemistry that supports the production of many materials, made complex calculations for the navigation of the seas.

As with many islands, there is another island, of canals and pools hiding in plain sight. As business is conducted above lives a few meters lower, at the surface of the water take place, busier and more human than the abstracted designs and plans above. It is not secret however, but rather overlooked as unimportant in the face of problems posed and solved. But the wealth of the island such as it is, is not reflected in the tall towers, stone foundations, and great cables that monumentalise the island, but in quiet peaceful lives of those underneath them. They have few problems of their own as long as they solve the problems of others.

Pirates.

They tried to board the ship.

There were screams from above,
Then silence.

She came in soaked with blood and seawater.

You smelled it before you heard her sit.

She dropped a blade on the floor.

Clattering in the dark,
then you heard her breathing. Long, ragged pulls.

You didn't ask what happened.
You didn't ask who won.
You reached for the bandages.
You tend to her.

Voids.

Even at a distance it looks like something is missing. The island seems interrupted on the horizon. It's hard to describe an island, it's shape and then to say but there's a bit missing. Especially when it's an irregular shape. It's easy to spot a corner cut from a cube, or a slice from a sphere, and yet when looking at the island…. Something is gone, there are many things gone.

There are great empty spaces defined by the island of voids, not only empty spaces – but absent ones, not only absent spaces, but all manner of absent things. One end of the island has an outer edge that defines a crater sunk into the sea bed, the crescent of a former volcano takes another edge. Houses can be found, none ever complete, doors miss handles, or doorways doors. Sometimes a roof or wall has gone, but never enough to stop the house from remaining more house than not.

The topology of the island itself is defined by gaps, forests defined by clearings, trees by hollows, mountains defined by crevasse or cave, the cave by an inaccessible flooded chamber, crevasse by one last fault in the bedrock, lakes around their whirlpools, rivers by a space round which the waters run where there should be a boulder rested in the silt, but there is not. While all these things may be present in nature, here they stand out as voids.

It becomes clearer in the smaller scale. The spider's web has one strand missing, the tuft of grass is less than blades, the grains of sand running through your fingers on the shoreline are not numerous enough to measure the time it takes for them to fall. Less sand than stars.

However what conspicuously defines the island the most is the sound it makes. A shifting hollow mournful song, heard by the sound waves against the shore, the rain on its surfaces, And the wind as it plays the island itself like an instrument. Each void the island presents, the weather plays like an instrument. But again the melody is lacking, a few notes unplayed, some instruments untouched.

As for those who live on the island, there are not enough. One child, one parent, one partner, one elder too few... lives lived conspicuously without certain gestures, habits and rituals. A person may walk a path – and leave a space beside them, their hand lingering at their side without another to hold, without a shoulder to brush against, without an ear to listen to everyday words. Houses without places set at tables, double beds with only one pillow, rooms without furnishings. Children play games without participants.

But no void is ever acknowledged, if it were, it would be there.

Vaults.

The sea is quiet here, still for miles, the island is a patch of cold volcanic black. Long ago when the world was afraid of the future, they started to hoard things. Usually individuals who imagined some cataclysm that they could wait out in silos. Storing only what they and their chosen nearest would need. An act of essentialism and survival for an undetermined but limited amount of time. None planned to be underground forever. Others took an altogether different view, they imagined after the end, and imagined if not a restoration of, but a gift to the world to come from the past. A message in a bottle, where the message itself was something tangible. They saved seeds.

Every known plant was sourced, and the small tough sleeping children were sealed and stored underground. Not all these were successful, some failed before the waters came, wrecked by a lack of investment, earthquakes and accidents. Some flooded. But one survived. There was enough foresight that its location was high, dry and cold, and when the waters came it remained so. Its remoteness and the barren rock around it held off early migrants looking for landing sites. Then later, coincidence played a part in its survival. The guardians of the vault had time to arm and defend themselves, but they were aided over time by the arrival of a different migrant to make their mark.

The island is a shallow pile of slate, scattered with dots of stained white. These are mostly snow, except these patches will on occasion move. Great polar bears stalk the island, and not just a single family. When the waters removed their nearby habitats, the world's remaining polar bears set out, those that survived found themselves stranded here, in their hundreds.

Their behavior has changed from solitary males and females, to family units, they hold territory but also common ground on beaches, with a shortage of food, they have also turned pack hunters, fishing in and out of the water by some distance.

Unguarded visitors soon found themselves prey, but it was not long before more organised human parties came to hunt till they were warded off by not just the bears but the guardians of the vault, and so began a mutual cooperation. The bears would guard, supported by the humans, and the vault would provide heat, shelter, fresh water.

Over time a complex and subtle set of behaviours have emerged between the two resident populations of the island. There are rituals of introduction to new children and bears. Infants left exposed for short periods of time in the presence of the bears which seem to take interest and patrol until parents return. Each aging generation of humans and bears are buried in the same area. The islanders will often keep the bodies of their dead, mummified and stored with the seeds, to await a companion bear's death. The bodies then placed together in the open, with humans and bears alike demonstrating grieving over the exposed bodies before burning. There is no attempt at domestication, but there is equivalence. Shares of Fish caught are left for the others, by both parties.

From this protected position, the islanders have invited select ships to come, and are sending out seeds into the world, to the islands with the capacity to grow again. Seeds are planted by the Captains of these ships, on the fertile islands, but also those most remote, the most resistant to human occupation, or just any location that may go unnoticed. We should not know about efforts to save the world, we would only spoil them.

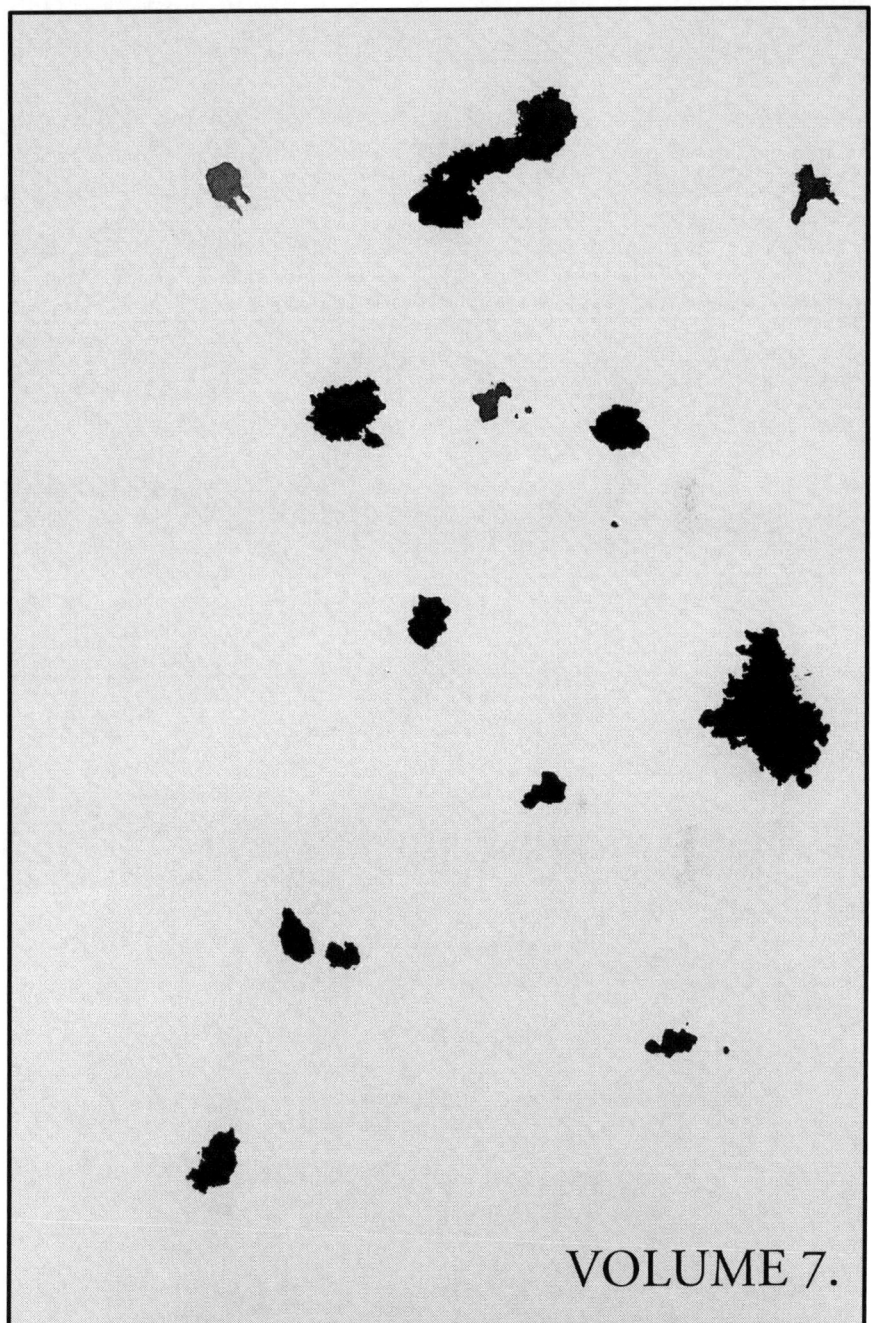

VOLUME 7.

Another Voyage.

On rare occasions you catch the Captain in your cabin half asleep.
You wake and hear them breathing.

You cross the room and find them slouched, exhausted.
Folded in the waxed skins and bandages they wear.

You have shaken them awake,
To check they are not injured.

Most times the Captain simply begins to recite an island.
But this time you do not ask about islands,
Or the Captain's health

You ask where the Captain is going,
And the Captain begins to talk as if to themselves.

'This is not my last voyage, I have one more…
There is an immortal jellyfish,
It never dies, it makes itself pregnant with itself,
Grows a new version of itself within itself,
The Same nervous system living briefly in two conjoined bodies,
Before the outer body sheds away.

I will leave the ship, slip seaward, float.
Imagine what I am to become.
I will feel the new life starting around my heart.
The beat will slow,
A net tightening around my chest.
The heart is the muscle that will unravel,
And begin myself again.

I will find it hard to breathe and I will sink.
Into the depths,
Lower with my last breath, bubbling up from my mouth,
Lower into the cold calm silence.
Pain shoots down my limbs,
Water floods my lungs,
my body convulses as I drown.

Round my heart a new skin is forming.
As my eyes glaze over, blankly marble stare,
New eyes open in the last warmth of my old body.

Fish come to see, they sense the new life,
Trapped inside and want to help.
Small fish at first, small bites, my
Fingers are chewed and nibbled at.
Then a passing squid wraps tentacles around my hand,
With its beak prunes my fingers like roses,
Blooming cold blood for the sea.

The frenzy starts as my body reaches the ocean floor.
A thousand silver shards dismantling the shell,
Crabs join the throng to rip apart the corpse
A storm of sediment, and ribboned flesh.

All that will be left is the crumbling rib cage,
From which I will unfurl anew.
Remade for the endless dark and deep,
Allowed forget the surface world,
And be taken by the ceaseless currents'.

VOLUME 7: ISLANDS.

Ghost.

The Captain sailed right through it. So rushed below, woke you, and hauled you up to the deck, then steered the ship around to make a reverse approach.

The Captain described it they sailed – but unlike the other islands where the Captain would press something into your hand as proof, or bring an island resident on board, or guide you onto the deck of the ship to smell and hear the island, the life, it's clamour – here there was nothing but their words. The motion of the ship was that of progressing through the open ocean, spray and a strong wind. Yes, those were the sounds of our vessel, the wind as it moved over us, the rush of low waves, parting at the bow. But nothing else.

And as for what the Captain saw, there was no other proof. This is why you were so urgently brought to the deck. To prove to the Captain, as much as prove to you, that it was there, as if your presence alone, even if unable to see, was enough for validation.

They said it was an island of air, resting in the sea; and they had sailed right through it. It had not seemed substantial enough at a distance to steer around, not even a cloud, barely a mist, and closer in it was too late, and in any case it merely resembled a strange formation of vapours, a collection of subtle colours. On the first approach the Captain had thought to cautiously hold their breath, and keep an eye on the birds resting on the bowsprit. But soon they gasped, and looked on open mouthed.

You circle the island, make passes through it. Every time the Captain spoke less and less, not so much as there was less to describe. But more so that the Captain was gently awed to silence.

In the vapour, suspended, they described an island of light. low Geography, a running river, abundant trees and vegetation. As real birds flew past on migration, you passed the softened ghosts of birds, resting on nebulous branches. The boughs bore fruit, of various types, and scuttling creatures, rodents or mammals it was hard to tell were at work in the undergrowth, harvesting and eating whatever had fallen. Up in the canopy here and there, some kind of monkey, with a long agile tail worked at dislodging a stubborn fruit from the grip of the tree. You exited the cloud, the Captain swung around on a different course.

The estuary of the river, the Captain sailed up it, to the island's interior, but now with the wind at our back against the flow of the river that wasn't there. He described freshwater fish, white and gold, rapids of churning froth and flows like glass. Upstream the river widens and shallows, and there in clearings a few shaded meters back, sits a village of bamboo walls and dry leaf roofs. Pathways are trodden and worn into the dirt. Plants are growing around the bases of the structures. You can see where the structures have been repaired with fresh mud. The village is active, there is wood being cut, food prepared, and various useful items being made, maintained or repaired. A child is being washed from a bowl, a mother talks to her daughter while root vegetables are cut, a grandfather watches everything while slowly eating rice, two men telling stories while knitting rope, a child pets a domesticated cow. There is no commotion or noise, but the village seems blissfully focussed on its own creation. Every action and look is a choreography of unfolding, leading to some small reveal of life.

While you sailed, you caught initially onto the excitement, the Captain described, and you committed details to memory, you asked questions. Was it the ghost of somewhere past, an island projected from somewhere near, a vision of the future, or one from another reality entirely? The details gave us clues, and this is what you think entranced the Captain the most, as you could hear them muttering between my questions 'They've not gone through it, this isn't here, their world isn't broken'. There were no remains from our history in the village, no plastic, rust, or glass. Nothing imported from another place, another time, the village and island had created each other, closely, carefully. But as the encounter drew on, the answers provided to your questions lost their drive, shortened, grew remote. Something had occurred to the Captain, an idea that disturbed them. The Captain at one point stated 'They cannot see us, we're not here'... and immediately a new course was planned, I asked for more and 'we've seen enough' was my rebuttal. The island had begun to haunt the pilot, and so they turned their back on it.

Skyscraper.

There are two islands at the same time, two sets of inhabitants. An island being destroyed, while another grows in its place. An island becoming a foundation, after being a scaffold; an island that was a shell, becoming the bones of a living being. Both these islands are one island, both sets of inhabitants the only inhabitants.

The island was and remains a series of skyscrapers, tall concrete and glass structures, bleached by the sun, salt worn, and soiled by whatever the sea threw against them. The glass has mostly gone, only a few windows remain, clasping the rich blue shades of the day and passing clouds.

Other windows hold onto their shards still. The very tops of the towers are pencil drawings of what they used to be. Just metal girders sketching out the memory of an architect's first thought. As floors and windows staircases, lift shafts come into view, the buildings flesh out. It is as if they fade into existence, dreamt downwards by the sky, not built up from the ground. Then as windows appear, sections of the sky are cut into squares and thrown back at you. If you turn around, you can see the sky they show you, undivided. There are voids. Where the glass has fallen away where the dark interior of a floor presents itself as a surface, less a hole, more a gap in reality, these are the spaces in the image of the towers that are most disturbing. The voids are less part of the ruin, more something emerging out of the ruin. Hints of places where there is no world at all, where the failure of our world reveals the possibility that everything might fail.

As your eye scans hurriedly down, birds fly into and out of the voids, puncturing them, making them real spaces again. The birds are nesting in unknown spaces, but real spaces nonetheless.

And, the infant young, once a year, parachute out, without silk, to learn to fly in a single tumble. And with the arrival of birds, single lines of ivy, stretch upwards and fan out around the tower, they follow cracks, in glass, in the lines of frames. They venture into voids and emerge from others unharmed. Deep green leaves, held by the rope like brown stalks, the rivers of life that anchor them to the building.

Here you see the first set of inhabitants, a speckled tide of humans clinging to the outside of the building. Attached by ropes and pulleys for safety, they move from section to section at work, in a way that you cannot tell from a distance what the work is. Bare tanned arms are outstretched over the surface of the tower, at the boundary of greenery, where it meets the glass. As you sail closer and set anchor, they will see you, and wave at you welcoming from the heights. When they turn back to work, the reframing of the body reveals more of what they are doing. They are guiding the ivy, trimming, tying and cultivating it to direct it into dense structured growth. They are not attaching the ivy to the skyscraper, they are growing it in parallel. A living lattice around and through the old building. Further down at the base, trees have been planted. They provide strength and support. The pillars of foundation. Each tree has also been shaped. Gargantuan Bonsai. At the initial branching off the trunk, the limbs are curved and interwoven to create cradles. Small pots of earth are imported from other islands and then lifted up and emptied here to create the ground from which a new tree can be grown atop another. Different trees are planted at different intervals to enable a viable structure; redwoods for major struts, willows for masses of knotted and flexible cord, tall thin but flexible poplars wind their way between or around the others. Ivy leads the way, the forward scout of this vertical forest, reaching up to outline the territory to be taken.

But there is a magic act taking place in front of you, at the base of the island. There is a second group of inhabitants tasked with a different line of work. A host of tiny soft hammer strikes, cable clips, and metal cut. If one walks between the trees at the base, there is no skyscraper. It has been chiselled away, till nothing but tree remains. Around you workers with brooms sweep away a fine dust that falls from above, and on looking up through the branches, layer upon layer, eventually you can see them working. They are eroding the ruined skyscraper from beneath and from within. A piece of stone or glass is chipped away in the dark, held in the hand, then against a hard coarse material it is ground away till only a dust remains. This is then brushed off hands and deposited like mist below. In this way the skyscraper is slowly and gently made to evaporate upwards, as the forest overtakes it, disappearing undercover, sleight of hand. Each day after work, they descend from the interior and brush down towards the base the remains caught on leaves and branches. They stow the diamonds they use for wearing down the building in pouches by their hips, worthless but for this function. They meet the gardeners from above who have abseiled down to meet them, and they rest and eat as one, before finding shelter in spaces made within. The skyscrapers to be are already here but will never be completed as they will always grow. But the skyscrapers they were, are already halfway gone, and blowing away on sea breezes day by day.

Confession.

You have altered the atlas.

Not on the page — there is no page — but in the rooms of memory where the islands live.

You changed the weather of one coast to match the mood you were in.

You gave a ruined tower light it never carried.

You moved a harbour mouth closer, because you could not hold the true distance.

The Captain senses it.

'You are not here to improve them,' she says. 'You are here to remember them.'

But memory is not still water. It shifts with each return, brightening what it favours, dimming what it despises.

You walk those internal halls again and find the shapes already warped.

So the confession is this: you cannot promise fidelity.

The atlas you keep is alive, and in living, it lies.

What remains is not their measure, but your measure of them.

Hospital.

The island was once a hotel. Tall and decadent, crowned with balconies and glass walls to reflect the sea. Now it is a hospital, and has been for some time. The glass is gone. Curtains flap in the wind where windows once gave views of wealth.

Only one part of the hospital truly functions: the maternity wing. It is the reason anyone comes.

People travel from all across the oceans, from broken islands and makeshift ports, carrying infants inside them like last hopes in fragile shells. They climb cracked staircases to deliver their future into waiting hands.

No one stays. The hospital grows wider, more ragged, more echoing every season. The birthing rooms move into former dining halls, then kitchens, then linen closets.

It is always expanding. There is always room for one more.

Reply.

island of
contestation?
sound

The wires on the horizon lead to pylons, the pylons to the island. Long wide flat grey beaches of slow wet sands prohibit an approach by water, you have to make a long walk ashore. There is an outpost that welcomes you, a hut stood uncertainly on posts sunk into the sand and sinking still. There is only the cold wind and the irritable crackling of the wires above to hear, there is little to see, and nothing moves, at least nothing moves at any pace. There is a procession of those making their way to the island in the distance, and a procession of those returning from it. Two Single file columns, facing in opposite directions, and seemingly immobile. But they do move. One foot at a time is lifted, peeled from the sand below, which relaxes its grip and softens, holding only for a second a footprint, before it is smoothed out. The foot hovers over the sand, a droplet of water gathers on the sole, forms, takes weight, reflects the world upside down and then falls into the sand below, the foot has moved barely a finger width from when the droplet started its existence to where it landed. The foot is extended and moved forward, so slowly, till it has extended just enough for a shift in balance to occur, and then it lightly descends, letting gravity press it to the sand once more, which lightens in colour as pressure moves moisture away, as grains are compacted to take a bodies weight. All of this so slowly, not for the sake of speed, but to lessen the sound: of footstep, of rustling clothing, of the granular grind of the and wet suction of the sand.

Each person in each line measures their steps, their movements, and even breathing, to remain unheard. To move so slowly as not to be seen to move. There is no consideration of speech, it is unthinkable. No one in living memory has spoken on the island, they come to listen. To approach the island in this way is an acclimatisation, a training for your time there.

Beyond the sands a single hard black rocky outcrop, and there dominating the sky is the dish. Smooth, dirty white and cradling the sky, a cup to hold the moon. Held in place by massive struts and gears that also enable its manoeuvre atop the whitewashed cube beneath. It's powered by the cables that run all the way from another island. The small protruding receiver antenna in the centre is poised to point in the exact direction of its target. A harpoon for clouds perhaps, in the imagination of children, but its reach is far more vast. It listens to the universe.

Those who approach come to listen, and the debt required is silence. Upon arriving at the island proper, there are two pathways running in concentric circles around the building. Those leaving those arriving. Entering the building each person finds a space, a seat upon the floor, some prefer to stand. There is a gradual rising and falling, a movement and rest as people find their places, as others begin to leave. Eventually when the room is full, the doors are softly closed. Nothing moves, and there is no sound. But the room must wait, as if lights were being raised at the theatre, from the auditory gloom emerge the faintest of sounds layer by layer. First a kind of acoustic background noise, the vibrations of the space itself, the movements of air, the mass of breathing, the vibration of the building from the live wires running through it, the distant tide humming in the sand till it brushes the island. Then details emerge, each person hears the people next to them, breathing, the micro movements of fabric, the sound of someone swallowing, their stomach churning, the cartilage of a single joint grinding. Soon the background noise can be isolated, drafts in the building are located, electricity picked out cable by cable, the echo in the high ceilinged space above.

Then somewhere a switch is flicked, the snap is like god clicking their fingers. A computer fan thrums, the hum of power rises, there are minuscule creaks of metal as the frame of the machine warms. Soft fingertips gently depress keys on the keyboard, each brush and warm plastic contact is felt. The sound of a screen warming. More typing. Then a hand is placed on a small dial. With the slightest turn, a further click, and the speakers begin an atmospheric earthquake, less heard than felt, all the air turbulent with energy. As the dial is turned the vibrations take a form… static.

Like the noise of the sand underfoot outside, a gradual granular mass of sound is conjured into the room. The volume is increased and it fills the space. An infinite number of footsteps on the sand, overlapping and indistinguishable. It is the sound of the universe. The dish is turned to the heavens and listens and receives every signal; every burning star and flare, each pulsar and black hole, every asteroid collision, every planet turning, meteors falling, all the radiation, light, and heat, the vibrations in clouds of molecular dust from the beginning of time, taken and translated into waves received by attentive ears. Tiny bones in skulls, dancing to a song originally sung at the far side of existence.

All in the room are focused, they listen to hear pattern, to hear exception, to hear an answer to questions asked, to hear proof of something more than this. Few are there to hear what is exactly offered, a slice of eternity. Some imagine that at some point god or the angels may simply declare themselves and speak – Or that out of the static a beacon signal may be heard, a broadcast from another earth, another world, another civilisation. Intentional or accidental, but a final end to the privileged loneliness of being sentient.

After a period of time each day, the signal is turned off. The listening brings many to tears, for many reasons. So the room is often filled with sob and cries that take the place of the static, till they too settle back to silence.

Doors are opened, the gentle substitution of bodies occurs. Stepping out, for departure, the experience of slowly and silently leaving the island past the incoming visitors and across the sands is its secret redemption. Each person passing can be heard, the ground and sand and sea and sky can be heard. The chorus of blood in your veins and the orchestra of your pumping heart, play for you.

Hostility.

If you can stay on the island for one night, find yourself a place to sleep, and last it out without injury or death, you are considered to have become a native.

The island was an island, long before the floods; now it is merely smaller. A green and pleasant home to its inhabitants, and though they prided themselves on their long history that extended into myth, the island had never been theirs to begin with. The island's real history was one waves of arrivals, one generation of another, each invited, each absorbed, each forgotten. At the end of each day, the cloak of myth would be pulled tight around those who slept on the island, and they dreamt that the island matched their dreams.

When the floods came new people arrived, but jealous of their home, they set to defending and rejecting all newcomers.

Cliffs were sharpened into knives. Brambles with the most barbed Thorns planted. Poisonous plants and fungi cultivated. Vermin and venomous animals, sourced and introduced. Pitfalls dug, traps, snares, and swing branches set, boulder falls rigged. Unstable buildings set to collapse, support from walls removed. The ground itself made untrustworthy, smoothed where grip was needed, loose pathway stones discreetly placed on cliff side paths.

The new inhabitants however were not to be removed, as what had been misunderstood was their own resolve to stay. Those *originally* on the island had little comprehension of the suffering and hardship that others had already been through. They had come from islands destroyed, states led by madmen, on journeys with no guarantee of survival shepherded by wolves.

The arrivals set themselves to surrender, not to the inhabitants, not by leaving, but by accepting the conditions of the island. The sharpened edges were to be nestled into, and rough stones set as gifts to toughen one's skin with. Thorns offered needles, and defences for their own homes. Traps defined the pathways. They did not withstand or survive the island, they offered themselves to it on its own terms.

Original inhabitants began to die from small exposures to the flora and fauna of the island that they themselves had established. Careless poachers caught in their own traps. Frustrated owners finding new neighbours in every place they thought they had made impossible. Eventually some of the originals started to leave. More died, and others hid themselves away as if they were not really there, as if the new form of the island had not taken shape. More left.

As for new arrivals, having lost everything, they took the island as they found it, picked up the tatters of the original islanders myth, and patched its holes and tears with the remains of their own. Now their fortitude gained from exile matched the islands, their survival tested by the island proved their worth, the hostility of the island defended them.

Now a new history of the island was restored, as while they had taken their place on the island, the original islanders had long since left. Now the living story of the island is that all are welcome, those who can thrive there do, and the myth of the island is that it is a story, made by those who arrive each day, and stay one night.

the islands change...

Abandon.

'You don't describe every island.'

You don't accuse her. It's not that kind of statement.

'No… Some islands don't want to be remembered,' she says.

'You mean you don't want to remember them.'

'Same thing,' she says.

You tilt your face toward her. 'You've brought me to them, though.'

'But we never landed,' she replies. 'Sometimes I just point. Sometimes that's enough.'

There's something in her voice, an edge.

'Would it hurt you, if you spoke them aloud?'

She steps past you. 'There are places to sail around. Not because they're dangerous. Not everything needs to be known.'

'And what happens if you forget them entirely?'

'Then they find someone else to remember them.'

You say nothing. The tiller creaks. Somewhere behind you, something falls, or is dropped, into the sea.

Burial.

Funerals and wakes are held elsewhere. It is jealously guarded by the communities of several islands, with patrolling boats. It is a piece of actual land, not a rock, or a building, or wreckage from before. It was a hill of earth, of no great importance in its day, but noticeable. In other places these remaining plots of land are prized as garden sites for food, with islands built around them the growth of hemp or corn or seeds, the central hub of a community that floats in orbit around it. Here the island is lonely, bare but for grasses and meadow flowers, and with only a few attendant ships and souls moored nearby. It is as if it has only just been discovered, cleared and prepared, and is awaiting the arrival of a caravan of inhabitants. But the island is fully occupied. A foot trodden path can be seen winding its way up the island, at the peak a small circle of stones outlines the entrance to a circular stairway descending into the hill.

The dead who have achieved wealth, power, influence, or fame are brought here. It is the only known devoted burial site. Bodies arrive by boat, wrapped tight in dried seaweed, glossy and smooth like butterfly pupae. They are handed over at mooring to bearers who, placing them on a white stretcher between their shoulders, walk the body along the path, circling up the island to the summit. The walk is calm, unhurried but not needlessly slow. It passes beds of flowers humming with bees and trilling crickets in the grass. The sea breeze buffets gently on the eastern portion of the island with prevailing winds and for most of the year, the sun is warming. Gull pass by overhead, the tides flow easily round the island, crest of waves are soft against the land. At the summit an unbroken horizon extends in all directions, and there is the peace that comes with seeing all the world from a high vantage point. And while the dead do not see this, the attendants taking the body, take in all these earthly pleasures on their behalf, surrogates for the final experiences. Then, once the sun has warmed their bodies, it sets, and the attendants wait for the last sliver of gold to vanish, but before the light has gone they descend the staircase into the interior. Level after level, one narrow corridor after another, cut into the sandstone bedrock of the island, and in every wall small chambers cut to lay a body flat, the air is cool and dry. There is no hierarchy in the catacomb, the next space empty is the next space used. The cocoon is placed, a hand is rested briefly on it, and then it is left, the attendants climb the stairs, descend the pathway under the stars, and push their boat from mooring, and the island is left deserted.

What is not known is that to maintain space in the island, bodies later are cut from their husks and removed, taken from the island via a cliff based cave at night. The bodies are stripped of consumable meat on the boat, and the fresh bones taken to another island for other uses.

but 'burial' is a deceit

Ice.

For the most part, the frozen islands are simply bleak outcrops from the slush covered in tents. The ice, filthy from the life chipping into its surface. Ice so full of dirt, it's barely ice. Beneath is, permafrost, frozen a millennia ago. Too hard to dig for the most part.

Some islands try, hacking and sawing frozen fertile soil to be thawed, moved and deposited elsewhere. Sold to islands that are looking to add a layer of productive topsoil.

Elsewhere are the blues and whites of frozen saltwater. The great expanses are gone, icebergs remain, but are left alone. With all too regular and alarming speed they can melt or flip without warning. Fatal for anyone clung onto one. So despite offering temptation as floating islands, they are phantoms.

Sometimes in the seas there are cold climates and freshwater, but this ice is too valuable a resource to spoil by residing on it, and is soon carved out and exported. Dry climates beg for ice.

Long ago there were glaciers where even older worlds, those before memory, were buried, crushed flat, and churned. Irretrievable and irreparable, mangled. The slow cold hammers of nature are gone now, but islands formed by ice remain through negative space; dwellings built into the high sides of valleys carved by absent glaciers. These are the islands of Ice.

All this is a prologue to the strangeness of this particular place. An island that appears indistinctly as a flat perimeter of powder snow-dunes in a sluggish partly frozen sea. Encampments of igloos can be seen just over the dunes, smooth manufactured curves blending with the windswept ones. Small thin spirals of occasional silken smoke threading upwards if a fire has been raised for cooking.

There is little life on display, too cold to linger between buildings, little work to do outdoors. So, once you have docked and made it past the eerily quiet and featureless dunes and shelters, you find yourself on a beach of snow, glaring in the light. As you squint you see your first real evidence of people. Light shadows in the snow, the imprints of footsteps converging into depressed pathways, marking the strides of those ahead of you. The snowflake sands descend and open out onto the incongruous view of a lake. A lake held within the sea, still and pure.

Then rumbling low, from the chill glass surface comes the scraping sound of metal. In the distance, scores of bodies, breath steam puffing from their mouths, arms wide, upright, are gliding in curves and circles. Heavy boots, fitted with blades allowing the islanders to skate across the lake, which is frozen solid.

The lake is not just frozen at the top, there is no risk of crack or falling through. This is a mountain of ice that descends to the earth deep below, and the water, the ice, is as clear as glass. The impression this gives is that the skaters glide upon an invisible surface above a dark and hollowed out quarry of ice. Each day the islanders skate and carve traces in the surface, but at night a team of dedicated workers come out to smooth and polish the surface again, to maintain its perfect transparency. Each day, morning and evening, the islanders return to conduct their social lives while appearing to effortlessly glide through space.

Of course there are other places one could skate on ice, but here the experience is completely different. Due to the hard polish of the ice, skating here feels like flight. Especially on cloudy days, when the angle of the sun or diffuse light denies reflection, and the skaters old and young traverse a huge expanse that seems to fall away, allowing you to look with perfect clarity at what lies beneath.

Here, there is one more wonder to behold here. Beneath their blades, beneath the ice, if one looks down, there is a city. Lit dimly from the light above, the spires of towers look like needles, the flat tops – stepping stones. Between them the light fades and it darkens to twilight, where treetops still preserved in darkest green stand tall but dead.

At street level there is no life, but automobiles are resting. At their windows there is a gleam, air trapped inside remains. When the waters rose and froze it was held there in perpetuity. It is presumed that when the world flooded, they rose around the city and then froze near instantly. How this happened is not known, that it did, is apparent. The ice is clear as glass. As such it is still possible to see the bodies of the frozen dead, held with balletic poise, clothing rippling around their torsos, trousers and skirts pressed against legs, coats and scarfs trailing behind. They have been captured while wading or swimming in the flood. Brought to a halt as the freeze set in. Many are just a footstep from the ground – reaching forward in one last attempt to escape, others drowning in convulsive poses look like they are dancing, those who are swimming appear as if in flight. Many have their last gasp of air, frozen in their mouth, or ascending just before their rigid eyes in one last mocking moment.

Far above, Children skate over the buried past, their blades only momentarily cutting the surface.

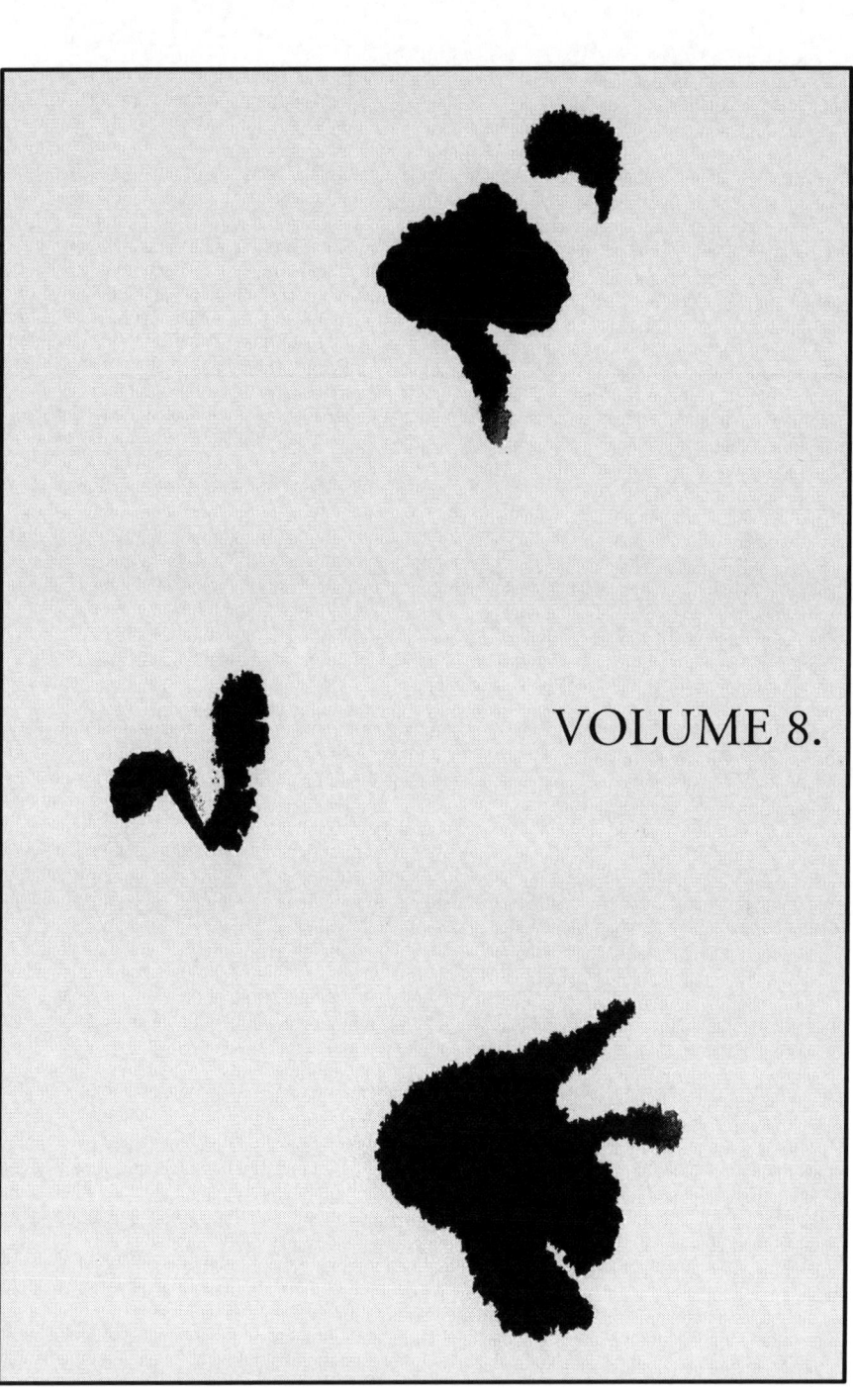

VOLUME 8.

Sight.

Slowly your body is recovering,
First you can stand, then you can walk,
You are still stumbling and full of pain,
The scar of the injury that broke you,
Is no longer tender,
A soft ridge,
Nerve endings mending,
You think you will soon unwrap your eyes,
To see the world again.
You plan to join the Captain on her voyage.

You start to have dreams,
Of a library at night.

A lofty zig-zag of a building,
Along the length of a high-sided valley,
Lush forest to the horizon.
The outer walls are smooth and white,
The floor is polished dark parquet.
Inside, on warping wooden shelves,
Flow rows upon rows of books,
In their thousands.

The library has no roof, so less a building,
More a crooked way with crooked walls,
Lined with books, all bound in leather.
In the dreams there are no clouds;
Just the sky,
Ice black, unbroken,
Reaching as far as the stars,

Who look down attentively,
As if to read every book that lays beneath them.

You dream that you have written all the books.
You dream that you have written none.
You dream you walk the corridor,
Between the looming stacks,
Of everything that can be written,
And think 'one more'.

VOLUME 8: ISLANDS.

Maelstrom.

The Captain pulls alongside another ship, and the Captain does not bring themselves below deck alone, they bring a guest. Their progress is slow, and the guests' breath rattles, they are careful. Uneven steps, guided to sitting. An offer of a blanket. When the Captain asks them to tell you where they have been, they speak in a tired aged voice.

'For all the waters pouring endlessly into the world, islands always remained, and so it stood to reason there must be ways for the waters to escape the world. I found one. There is a place on the map, where it all falls away. It can be heard first, then felt in the tide, then sensed in the air, then finally it can be seen. A whirlpool miles across, a swirling void into some immense other space... and people go there to discard objects, memories, to discard their lives.

They arrive on the horizon. Ships heavy in the water, at risk of sinking, capsizing, of being pulled into the maelstrom. People on the decks, have come with possessions, to hurl them into the vortex.

Approaching the maelstrom at a distance is considered a risk, as many a ship has been intercepted and hijacked in order for its contents to be looted. The pirates aboard those ships consider what they do a service, they are simply speeding the process of these items being discarded.

If you make it past the pirates, you dock by lashing your ship to one of four rocky outcroppings that surround it. That's where I found myself, attending to the ships that moor there. I was amongst a crew that would slowly extend the rope to take your ship to the edge, and once all was discarded, pull the ship back.

It is a remorseless place, screaming winds, the constant roar of the waters. Ships are turned to face the wind and tide, use their force to hold the boat down, so that the wind passes over it, rather than pick up the ship and toss it into the centre of the Whirlpool – like how a child throws a rock off a cliff, casually, with a desire to see how far it can go, and how damaging the landing will be.

When the ship is extended far enough, the passengers emerge on deck, and throw away the things that harm them most. It does not matter what they are, just things, held in their hand or arms, some dropped, some hurled. Sometimes the winds will take an object, and rather than falling into the waters, it will be carried in the air, mocking the person who let it go, refusing to disappear, circling chaotically above them.

Often I saw people do the same, step off the edges of boats and disappear, others carried in the tides for too long, not being taken in, not drowning, but carried with indifference until they collided with some other flowing wreckage.

Once a poor fool, who stepped out into the winds was hoisted kite like up and up, by the loose clothing they wore. Screaming all the while, but screaming quieter than the winds and waters. Then dropped into the centre of the maw.

I was there, three years, the toil, the loss of the world, it takes a lot.

Then we helped a ship, lowered it slowly to the edge. They stayed a while on deck. Then cut themselves loose. The whole ship…

I could not stay, so I took passage on the next ship out.'.

The guest was escorted from my cabin. The ships parted. The Captain rejoined me.

'We need not visit that place'.

Rig.

The men put on their most smiling, polite and welcoming voices. They will have brushed their hair, and washed their faces; even changed clothes, and whatever they think gives a good impression. But, they cannot hide the varied horrors of their surroundings. The sea for miles around, slow to move and rainbow sick with oil, the birds and fish dead upon the surface. Then the oil rig island itself, long since dysfunctional, remains stubbornly unchanged from a lack of vision. It is exactly as it was, a raised and mangled fist of metal, its wrist descending into the waters. All rusted paint, peeling and unrepaired.

Other rig islands are much better, they repaint, plant trees, welcome birds, clean the frame. They loose their moorings and slowly find fairer conditions, they rebuild what was broken with dried seaweed and papier-mâché; as they come across ships at sea they occasionally find new souls to add to the island life.

Not here. Only men, only the original men, growing old and strange live here. Beckoning on the balcony 'come here, come up, we would like to talk'. Few accept. Partially because the plea feels wrong, there is something desperate about them; partly the state of the rig and its surroundings. Mostly though it is the reputation of the rig that precedes itself, it is known that any women who step onto the rig never return.

Beside the rig is the disaster that led to its desertion and dereliction. A man-made disaster; a pipe dislodged, a spark, a near endless supply of gas ignited, the sea on fire. It resembles an eye, fringed with foam, steam rising. Beneath the roiling skin of water there is the orange glow of fire, a sun beneath the sea, sustained by the sheer pressure of its expulsion. The eye looks at the rig without remorse, and each day those of the rig avert their gaze and call for company.

Safety.

She said the deck was safe.

So you went.

Your hands found tar, frayed rope, dried fish scales.
The railings had been smoothed by time and salt.
Some parts of the ship hummed, others clicked.

You followed a sound to the stern —
not music, not voice,
but the steady rhythm
of something alive
and working.

You thought of it as the ship's breath.

Paper.

The glut of human knowledge is the foundation of the island, newsprint, magazines, novels from every pulp romance and crime, dystopian science fictions, instructional manuals for machines long gone, travelogues to countries and cities that are now sunk, advice for abandoned practices, school textbooks for subjects never to be studied again, the rules and secrets and stories of a vanished world. All gone.

In their place a grey lumpen island, smooth and undulating, built from the mash of language. Layer upon layer of text, ripped from its spine, ripped into strips, laid like new skin, dead upon its surface. On the whole little is read, not only are the words found here useless now, they were useless when written long ago.

This is not a library of classics, or of science and philosophy being churned for construction. This is the mass of forgotten and unremarkable print. The books that were still written and produced when machine intelligence was in ascendancy, but people still tried to write. The paper is the leftovers from a dead economy, landfill, overproduced, unrecycled. But waste has value. So now retrieved and mined from under the waters, literally dug from underneath submerged roads where it had been used as foundation for tarmac. Unsurfaced, resurfaced, dried and papier-mâchéd to form a new material world.

The paper is cheap, poor quality, but adaptable, so it is traded and supports other islands. Sometimes paper is sold to passing boats, there are ships that still make maps, or use the paper to manage repairs. What high quality paper they produce is often saved for library ships, which visit occasionally in search of raw material for their books, and exchange for valuable goods for it.

Writing has not died out here completely though, the island is home to a school of writers. However they only use and construct texts from what they find. The irony is that both the writers of the island and the writers aboard the Library Ships view each other with disdain. For those on the island there are no new words, here is no new world, everything has been written, any value left is to be found in the recombination of the old or existent. They hope not for truth, there is no unlocking, or discovery to be made here. They are simply exhausting the possibilities. Winding up the use of words.

Rust.

There is nothing here but rust.

A planet of orange. Dust drifts in heavy spirals, clinging to the air like breath made visible.

Every surface flakes to the touch. The ground crunches underfoot, not with leaves, not with gravel, but with layers of metal that have fallen out of time.

The buildings—if they ever were buildings—are collapsed skeletons of cranes and container shells, brittle as eggshells. The air carries a tang, like blood and battery acid. There is no water. No green. Just oxidation and the memory of industry.

The people here are coated in orange. They move slowly, speaking in a language of gesture. Some write messages in the rust, only for them to disappear with the next winds.

Library.

Briefly there were library islands, but soon it was clear that they were too precious to leave to the uncertain land. So the island of Library is a floating pontoon. Empty for most of the time, just rows of floating planks and rope handrails. Eight jetties, a tall central mast, attached to a strong chain and anchor beneath, with a long flag of golden reflective material. From time to time eight ships join the structure. Each ship specialises in a certain kind of text but holds a range of others that are considered essential.

Each ship is Captained by a librarian, then the sailors. Each ship has a writer in residence who writes a life-book of the ship itself. Sometimes those aboard will write additional texts depending on their specialist knowledge, or transcribe the knowledge of people encountered. This is how libraries now differ from those in the past, they move, and they do not focus on the storage, but rather the creation and distribution of books. Each ship receives visitations from other smaller vessels. Accounts are relayed and pulled together from the fragments and strands. Books are formed, version upon version, duplicated and shared.

The focus of the island is the networking of new texts, the mapping of journeys, regions not covered, texts needed by certain islands, text needed by certain library ships. In good weather, when the pontoons are full of ships, the jetties themselves are crowded with the bodies of the sailors. But where on other crowded islands there would be a hubbub of voices, here there is none. Not that it is silent. There is the constant slip and rasp of pages being turned, the soft slap and thud of books being passed or stacked. The librarians cluster around each other, looking over each other's shoulder, pointing to new texts, signalling in coded hand gestures for what they need above their heads. The orientation of the palm, the fingers extended, the thumb pressed to which part of which digit to indicate a lack or a surplus, a certain kind of text, new or old, updated.

As the Captain describes the island, you realise that the ship you are on must be a Library ship, but one unlike all the others. There are no texts, only you. No knowledge written but for the fringe islands of the world.

While it is reported to the world ship, its accounts are shared wide across fiction, food, life and survival.

Theatre.

Some islands make little sense, mostly because their origins are obscure, or for some the way in which they operate or survive, some it is intentional.

A large rocky outcrop, possibly a mountain or large hill top, plateaued. It is clear that ground works are underway, a small number of dedicated workers, mostly women, toolbelted, in leather aprons over sensible outdoor clothing, but casual enough to reveal they've long been at the work and do not mind the elements. The tools at hand indicate the nature of the work, carpentry.

A mountain top Theatre. What stories need to be acted out in person? The theatre itself is embedded in a circular frame island floats in a circle rotating. It is a stage. The building looks like a giant misshapen dice, a count of sides makes ten, so it would be a dodecahedron if not for various additional carbuncles.

In some ways the island resembles a prototype of the stilted city known to make its way through the oceans. But while it's… external build seems more rudimentary and stable, this belies its ability to transform. It is called the theatre. Quite why is unclear, if the etymology is either from a playhouse or surgical as neither operation is conducted.

There are periodic 'events'. Those who live on the island climb into the interior of the shape, and then 'guests' are invited by ladder to climb within. After a series of winding black wooden corridors, the viewer will find themselves inside a large auditorium of sorts. The walls are wooden panels, the shape of the room irregular, with dips in the ceiling and the floor, curved and angles in the walls. There are no windows, the only lighting provided by large collections of sturdy metal lamps with candles inside. But even these leave large sections of the chamber in darkness, and throw disorienting shadows. It is hard to know where to stand or sit, but people find themselves doing so, and in the empty space and burning light the viewers themselves become objects of observation. Each person their own portrait, each group a tableau to be considered. The lack of details in the space draw your attention to localised minutia. While the space is clean, between boards dirt has accumulated, and with use the boards themselves are polished smooth, there are scratches and gouges in the wood, that invite exploration. If one finds a fragment of thread, cloth, metal, stone it feels as if you have discovered some ancient remnant, a piece of treasure.

Then in the lull, the event begins. A rope will be lowered from the ceiling and sway. Then a board in a wall, will detach and lean out to reveal a fan of canvas behind it. A section the floor will lift creating a platform. If a viewer is stood by any of the psd as they occur, they either move out its way in surprise, or resolve to hold their ground and watch at close quarters. In turn they become framed in relation to the movement of the room, their presence and the room's manoeuvrings become one. No fictions are enacted, the theatre is only one show, and what is being shown, is undefined.

Each morning there is an opening of the sides of the building, wooden walls are removed leaving only five large internal struts in place to hold the two halves apart, moving the curtains open to the horizon to await the sunrise. All involved who will have slept on the stage or in the seating, will wake each other, and walk through the proscenium arch across to the back of the stage to watch the sunrise.

Down below on the edge of the island are a terraced row of houses, whitewashed with great slate roofs, thick walled and, recently built additions to the island. Built by its occupants, for functionality, a place to sleep and rest away from the work in the theatre above it. If you ask them if they work within the theatre, all will deny it, or any understanding of what happens within.

VOLUME 9.

Escape.

You have asked the Captain so many times
About where she came from.
How she came to find the ship.
She has never answered.
Then one night.
Before the islands, without request,
She simply starts to tell you.

'I was born on a fairly small and unremarkable island. Huts and
rocky outcrops, some dirt, some plants, fishing economy. The island
had a kind of puritan approach to life and these extended from
their religious beliefs, out their understanding of the world, and to
what people should be.

Since the fracture, the waters around the island were weird, strange
fish, colored tides, light seeping in through the cracks in the sky.
Mutations of the population of the island were common, and they
were not tolerated. On the island, everyone would wear gowns that
covered most of your skin. Limbs wrapped in bandages. This was
ostensibly to protect the purity of the body from the weirdness of the
waters. But, what most of the people of the island were doing was
hiding the growths, the distortions, and other strange effects that
the waters had on their bodies. It created a paranoid atmosphere
where everyone was talking and acting and as if they were
untouched, when pretty much everyone on the island was corrupted
in one way or another.

If there were a petty dispute, it was a simple enough thing to accuse
the person you wanted to punish of corruption. Their body would
be unwrapped.

There would be some kind of trial and an execution would take place. This was commonplace.

Now, the island would often trade with passing ships. Many prized that the island presented itself as pure. So while the crops we grew on the island were meagre, they were of value.
Some of the ships that would come to the island to trade were plague ships. These always ran particular flags, and often looked fairly similar to the inhabitants of our own island, wrapped in bandages. Though theirs would often be stained and dark, weather worn. Tradable goods would be sent out on small boats, unmanned and pulled by ropes, and exchanged for whatever the island was short of. These would be sent back to be quarantined and purified before anybody touched them on the island.

As I grew up, I became aware that I too was corrupted like everyone else on the island, but it was a particular kind of difference that it seeped into my body, one that I wasn't horrified by, one I am frankly mystified by, but have come to love… In any case, as I grew up on the islands there were men, and men that took an interest in me, and men that I did not want to be interested in me… Any physical contact would have revealed my so-called corruption. Over time my rejection of men on the island became noticed, and they became resentful.

I had planned my departure from the island for some time. I had constructed a boat, not this one, a smaller more modest craft. How I came by the craft is an entirely different tale. I hid it in a small cove. I was planning a long journey, I planned to depart according to my own schedule. Unfortunately, some of the islanders weren't running to my schedule. They came to my shelter, and there was an incident. They had underestimated my strength, and my determination not to be detained by them. They came to my shelter that night, and they did not leave. At that point it was clear I had to. I took the few belongings I had. I took them to the boat and I left. Now the islanders, they discovered what I had done very quickly. They set out in their own boats when they realized that I was no longer on the island.

But I had camouflaged my boat as a plague ship. I had disguised myself in the rags and bandages of the afflicted. Some days after leaving the island they found me. Approached my improvised boat with caution. My disguise was perfect, I could see their revulsion. I told them I had seen nothing and heard nothing. I said they were welcome to come aboard, to search. I told them I was happy for the company and the conversation. Nothing was more horrifying to them than the offer of close company of someone so corrupted. They declined and let me go.

I have not had direct contact from the islanders for many years now. But they have not forgotten, they are still looking. They don't know I am the Captain of this ship. They don't know what happened to me. Once in a while, I've seen their ships docked at other islands or in the distance. But because of what I do with this ship and the reputation I have fostered, rarely do they approach me either.
In one respect, I have been and always will be on the run from my own island. There is no home for me to return to. I do not think another island will ever be home to me.'

With barely a pause she begins to describe another island.

VOLUME 9: ISLANDS.

Balloons.

Ghastly in the sky. Great misshapen skins of plastics, webbed with netting, lurching into the air, roped together. Clusters connected by wires that slacken and snap tight as each balloon drifts together and apart.

Suspended beneath each balloon are the carriages, lightweight cages of seaweed rope, containing people – and at the centre of each the burners, the fires that keep the balloons aloft. Sometimes a literal fire, a stove, or engine, a chemical reaction. Atop some Balloons are Propellers, ridiculous contraptions of spinning polished driftwood, skimmed thin, and sup. In the hopes of providing lift, or when attached to a carriage direction.

The mass of balloons bob and rotate in the sky over the horizon, sagging, filling, like exposed lungs in a cracked open rib cage under surgery, gasping for life, while the islanders crawl over and underneath them, attempting to maintain flight. Ants in the rib cage trying to keep the body alive.

Beneath the bulk of the Balloons, ropes hang down, the scrap of land beneath a workshop for the city above. There is shame attached to whosoever has to descend to take something for a balloon to stay aloft.

The population starve themselves, weight is the enemy, people look for smaller partners. Abstinence in consumption and minimalism in possessions are valued. They maintain a strong oral tradition of song and story telling, stories passed virally from one balloon carriage to another. Alongside great choral symphonies of improvised melodies. They tell stories of flight and departure, of birds, and kites, seeds on the wind, rockets and missiles. While the Balloons go nowhere, the song unbroken on the island soars day and night, whispering in the snow, murmuring at night, bellowing with sunrises, shrieking with storms. The song rises and falls as the island does.

While the island is visually grotesque, it is the last song, and the most hopeful song left in the world. A song that believes it can lift the world.

Render.

To describe the island, whales must first be explained. Whales were nearly lost, and then after the fracture the waters rose and they were left alone, weird waters led to strange fish. The whales recovered their numbers, the whales became assertive in their defence of territory and life in the face of humansi.

As the whales recovered, some humans tried again in ships to hunt the whales. But their behaviour had changed, with greater numbers, larger pods, and with the effect of the waters. It was not that whales had become aggressive, but they had become definitively and decisively intolerant to being hunted. And so as the stories go, when we attempted to begin the hunting of whales again, boats were swiftly and collectively targeted for destruction.

If a single whale were harmed, a common song would be heard from beneath the surface and the remaining pod of several whales would breach to launch themselves onto the hunting ships, obliterating our now more fragile craft.

Very few survivors were left from such attacks, even the remaining modern ships should be left burning and sinking from sustained assaults. Whaling is no longer a reward that is worth its debt.

Which brings us to 'Render'. Fat, oil and grease remain essential and highly valued commodities. The island that could process such materials would be a source of great wealth. The cooking vats of 'render' became that location. The island had once been an industrial town, now mostly submerged, but the machinery and metal from factories had been salvaged up the slope from the sea, to create a steep tangle of steel emerging from the sea.

Pluming smoke from its tall chimneys and an awful stench from great distances.

The sea approaching the island has a second golden layer on its surface. Small pools of oil, and soft white bubbles of fat float liquid on liquid. They soften the sound of the ocean, waves do not crash on the island shores, nor spray froth against the sides of boats. There is only the heavily unctuous slop and slap of oil containing the energy of the sea beneath it.

Great masses of congealed fat and oil from the world are sought out from the sunken sewers and pipelines of the world. In many cases teams of working sailors, freedive with rocks, the depths where in amongst the wreckage of the old world they dig up disintegrating roads and buildings to seek out coagulated waste to bring the surface in berglike lumps.

These are dragged to the shores of 'Render', pulled up the half sunken jetties, to be dissected by its workers. As such the inhabitants of 'Render' are dressed in thick sharkskin hides to keep themselves clean, but their outfits are adorned with barbs, spikes and hooks, to give them purchase wherever they go. The island is so replete with grease, there is no unoiled dry point. So boots with spikes drive deep into the ground, and the rough skin provides grip.

Inhabitants of the island, position their living quarters on ladders. Simple huts, raised the height of a person above the ground, amongst the machinery. This is so that their daily work clothes are hung out, dry, beneath their houses. They climb down into their clothes, and up out of them each day. Exposure to fat and grease cannot be prevented, and this over time amongst the elderly leads to a darkening and thickening of their skin to appear more leathery. This is well known and visible, as when not working, to limit their exposure, the islanders remain naked. At a distance the activity of the island gives a strange impression that each day its inhabitants descend a few meters to become clumsy half formed creatures, and then ascend again in the evening to become graceful naked humans. Each day they make this choice.

Leviathan.

Some islands are not islands, some things cannot be contained within a category. Some things, while new, feel like they must have existed before everything else. Before category, before description. How does one begin to describe a new-born god?

It is most often seen and described as a spherical mass of living flesh, an amalgam of every feature of every seaborne living creature and more; pulled apart, melded and warped together across its shifting surface. A row of shark fins, a field of crab claws. Here an eyelid rolls back to reveal a compound of giant squid eyes, arranged like those of a fly's. There an orifice opens to reveal the circular rings of a gigantic eels mouth, rows of teeth after teeth, but rather than eat, it pulses, to eject spray as if from the blowhole of a whale.

It is larger than many islands, but mobile. Emerging from and descending beneath the surface of deep seas without pattern. Frequently its expected spherical shape is defied by unfoldings of limb-like masses, or iceberg-sized masses linked by tentacular tethers.

when one is satisfied that it is a living thing, sections of it give way from flesh to tougher shell, these have molluscs, coral and seaweed clinging to the surface. Within these landscapes it is unclear if it becomes something geological, with wet sand and rock marbled with veins of mineral taking the place of flesh. Also the sea-water does not always seem to be running off the surface, as much as emerging from valleys and channels, as if the creature were a freshwater spring itself.

The scale of the creature is unbelievable, a ship can harbour in a fold of its hide. Its fecundity inspires awe. At times it has been witnessed that great chasms open in its flesh to seemingly birth pods of adult whales. At other times it sloughs off beds of coral, like a landslide, or a sea-wall of ice falling into the sea.

Not always benign or benevolent, it has been known to ignore attacks and substantial attempts to destroy it. At other times it seems to seek out and to consume ships whole, people have walked safely on its surface for days, while others have been quartered by razored tentacles flicking from beneath its skin moments after placing foot on it.

Is it old? Is it the first creature? Was the map of evolution wrong? Is it new, a seed pod of life? Is it an aberration? Is it alien? Is it the sea monster referenced in every ancient text? We cannot know the answers to the questions now, though we may ask them. But we may witness it.

Farm.

Once, the island sang with turbines. Blades turned in sync with the sky, summoning electricity from the breath of the world. Now the towers remain, but their arms are still—silent sentinels without purpose.

But the people have returned.

They have strung ropes between the towers, tight as harp strings, some woven thick, others looped like spider's silk. Hanging from these ropes are nests, woven homes like bird cradles, dangling and shifting in the wind.

To reach them, one must climb.

The wind returns in gusts. When it does, the homes sway.

Ridge.

The idea is simple, dig a hole in the ground, and use the dirt to create a ridge around the hole that keeps the water out, just like you can do on a beach. Then, build your houses and your life upon the ridge itself overlooking the sea. You have created a circular city, the island of Ridge.

When there's no more room on the ridge… dig deeper, start a new ridge, a short distance out behind where you are. Move your houses to the new ridge. Dig up the old ridge, and dig deeper to make a bigger hole and start work on the next ridge, in preparation for the next move outwards, repeat forever.

The first ridge was a tall imposing mass of earth, but a small circle. Each new iteration has since expanded the circumference of the island, but to save on resources the ridge has been a little lower, a little closer to the water's edge. Each time the island expands, the size of the ridge itself becomes smaller and smaller, less and less, stretched out and thin. But the line cannot be permitted to break or fragment, lest the waters flood in, fill the interior and ruin the chance to dig again.

The ground inside the circle is a pit of mud and rock, a constant clawing at the ground. Each generation of the island spends longer digging, each iteration of the island requires a longer dig, and more work to build and move the homes. The current iteration of the island was completed before the current digging generation was even born. The expansion of the island is a story handed down, from one generation to the next.

But now each generation feels less inclined to dig, a lifetime of work for a life that is not your own. Slowly the inhabitants are becoming idle, they will not work to build a new ridge, and as disaffection grows, people are leaving. Where once the ridge was dense with human life, there are now sections more like ghost towns. Ramshackle houses, empty of families. Also sections of the ridge are unfinished, merely a line of dirt, struggling to keep its head above the sea. The next iteration of ridge will take decades to complete, if it is completed. The next iteration will barely have any born to the island, if any at all. It will pass from existence like a slow ripple caused by a stone dropping in a lake. The sea will overtake its border, fill the interior, and return to pristine calm.

Air.

Each day starts a flat and crumpled rainbow. People sleep in the multicoloured folds, the bodies and breath keeping them warm within the plastic. Dew forms on the outer surface and pools. The first limbs carefully emerge, climbing out into the cold air to gather up the water. Somewhere an engine roughly coughs to life, then settles chugging to power the first of many fans. The rush of air that makes the island what it is.

One engine after another, succeeded and drowned-out by each and every fan. Folds are pushed out by air, pressure builds, the surface of the island begins to inflate. Rivulets of water stream down the rising lurid colours breaching upwards. People rolled out of ballooning structures, putting out their hands or cups to gather a morning mouthful.

Soon, structures take shape, evolving from each concertinaed mass, a playground forms; obstacle courses, tunnel networks, slides, and many, many, bouncy castles. Out from underneath the rising amusements the ground of disintegrating tarmac is revealed, broken, hardened dry. The inflatable island is ready.

Ships from all around gather with their children. The last great playground in the world. Sun bleached colours, swaying architecture, and the hoots and laughs of children. The island smells of a constant flowing mix of hot plastic, fumes from the engines, fresh sweat and salt. There is an ever present low rush of air, powered by the repetitive chug of the engines hidden away. The air whooshes into every looming, creaking structure, and finds its way out through safety vents, and gaps in the seams. Children run from one gaudy swaying cathedral to another. Launching themselves onto each new discovery with glee, and feeling the thrill of launching their bodies through space without fear of injury. At the same time exhausted children gather in heaps both in the shade provided outside, but also inside the structure. Laying prone while others bounce and lurch around them.

On closer inspection one can see guide ropes, pinning the inflatables to the ground, metal spikes driven deep. The inflatables themselves are also tended to, there are melted surfaces indicating repairs, stitches, patches of newer plastics, of slightly different shades. And if there should be a collision of bodies, a lost child, there is someone who comes to help. It is the rabbits that run the island.

Seven rabbits, each over six feet tall, patrol the island. With ever present toothy grins, and never blinking glistening eyes they greet each child. They wave, and offer hugs against their air filled puffy plastic skin. The Rabbits dance, it is a slow repetitive movement they bounce from left foot to right foot, tilting outstretched arms up and down as if waving long distance slowly with clarity. These inflatable island mascots circulate the island, following the mass of children as they move from inflatable to inflatable. They are silent and benign. But if you stand close, the smell of sweat has been ingrained into the outfits, you can hear the gasping of the person inside the suit, hot, breathing their own air. Sweated-out the figures inside the outfits must be exhausted, thin, desperate creatures. But no one sees them.

Guesswork.

She placed the sail in your lap
and the needle in your hand.

Said, "It doesn't have to be pretty.
Just tight."

You find the tear by feel,
pull the thread through the rough canvas.

Each stitch is a guess.
Each knot is a promise.

When you finish,
you know it will hold.

Weapons.

First indications are the remnants of former islands, flooded craters, waves lapping over the edges, the ragged broken rock outlines of islands, crime scene chalk marks in the sea.

The waters become shallow, and then you come to a constructed zone of inaccessibility. Sea mines bob at the surface, sulking as if denied the opportunity to hide, somehow both appearing heavy and buoyant. The dark heavy metal they are constructed from has been marked with paint, pairs of white X X marks, between the protruding prongs. They resemble eyes, staring out in confusion. You have to take an agreed upon route in and out from the island. As you approach, the number of eyes from the sea becomes a multitude.

Then the haze of orange arrives, the taste of metal in the air, the sea turns a muddy hue, Rust. The island emerges from it, a wall of metal hammered together, falling apart. At its core it remains solid, impregnable. But at every edge, it is corroding. Flakes fall into the sea, the wind scores dust from the surfaces and lays down salt for more erosion.

Here weapons are traded, made, refurbished and sold here. The primary product are guns, but there is also a line in the disarmament of the most dangerous and technically unusable armaments. These also serve as a means of defence for the island. large munitions are kept here but never sold. Only handguns, rifles, and machine guns. A monopoly on bullets is also maintained. The rest of the world works with bow and arrow, blade and cudgel.

The ownership of weapons brings pride and paranoia. So the island is defended by its own guns, the threat of the use of more alarming weapons. Then there is the Parade. around the wide battlements of the island, overseen from the central tower by its overseers, is a never ending procession.

A missile is held aloft, carried by four men. Behind them a heavy bomb is carted in a bespoke cradle. Grenade launchers, canisters of toxic materials, mines for land and sea, long range delivery systems are presented to the world. The men who make the parade, point these items to the outside world. Conducting a strange sideways crablike walk in constant surveillance of the out world. The parade never ends, night and day, in shifts, their self-satisfied and worried sense of power welcomes those who come to purchase some small item from them, or to dispose of something larger. Bit by bit all the weaponry of the old world that littered its remaining surface, finds its way here.

The island offers its own bleak hope, not that now people are any less inclined to fight. Just that those who wish to profit from this have isolated themselves, have made themselves conspicuous, and have built an edifice due to collapse…

Someday the whole place might just explode. One apocalyptic wiping clean. How long can the bomb in storage resist detonation, how long before human error arrives, how long before time degrades a component and natural reactions take place. A spark, a failure to separate, a bonding of elements, leading to a reaction and a transformative release of energy. Perhaps one day there will be a series of coincidences, a person in the wrong place, an object misplaced, a distraction, all leading to a simple misstep…

While all eyes on the island, marching sideways, are turned towards the horizon, there will one day be a wave of light, heat and pressure, from within the boundaries of the island. So swift and immense they will not know it has occurred, the speed of thought too slow against expanding chaos at their backs. The result of which, a happy obliteration.

Islands around the world will feel it; a distant rumble, large waves upon the shore, a change in weather, strange for the season. Fish will ripple unevenly in the shallows, birds will take flight as precaution. But the end of the world won't happen twice. Waves will pass, clouds will drift away, the flora and fauna of the world will return to untroubled observation of the tides. But the parade will finally be over.

Ledger.

While you recover daily you do not keep a log of gains, only of losses shared, between the Captain and yourself.

Salt has split your lips,

You taste rust and rope during meals.

The Captain's voice has shortened to the bone of words.

She stumbles on the deck, no longer agile.

Sleep is hard, noisy, and brief. It feels like bad weather.

There is a burn across your shoulder from a rope line you thought was slack, pulled tight. It reminds you of the burns that have healed.

The Captain complains of a numbness in her right hand from years of work.

You have each taken on a list of pains and misalignments and called it seamanship.

Islands leak into the creases of your mind. Tar lives under the Captain's nails.

You have begun to dream you are the ship. Toiling through the sea. If there is a balance in this, it is not in your favour.

You try to add up what the voyage owes you and what you owe it.
The sum is not zero.

But you are days away from your sight returning…

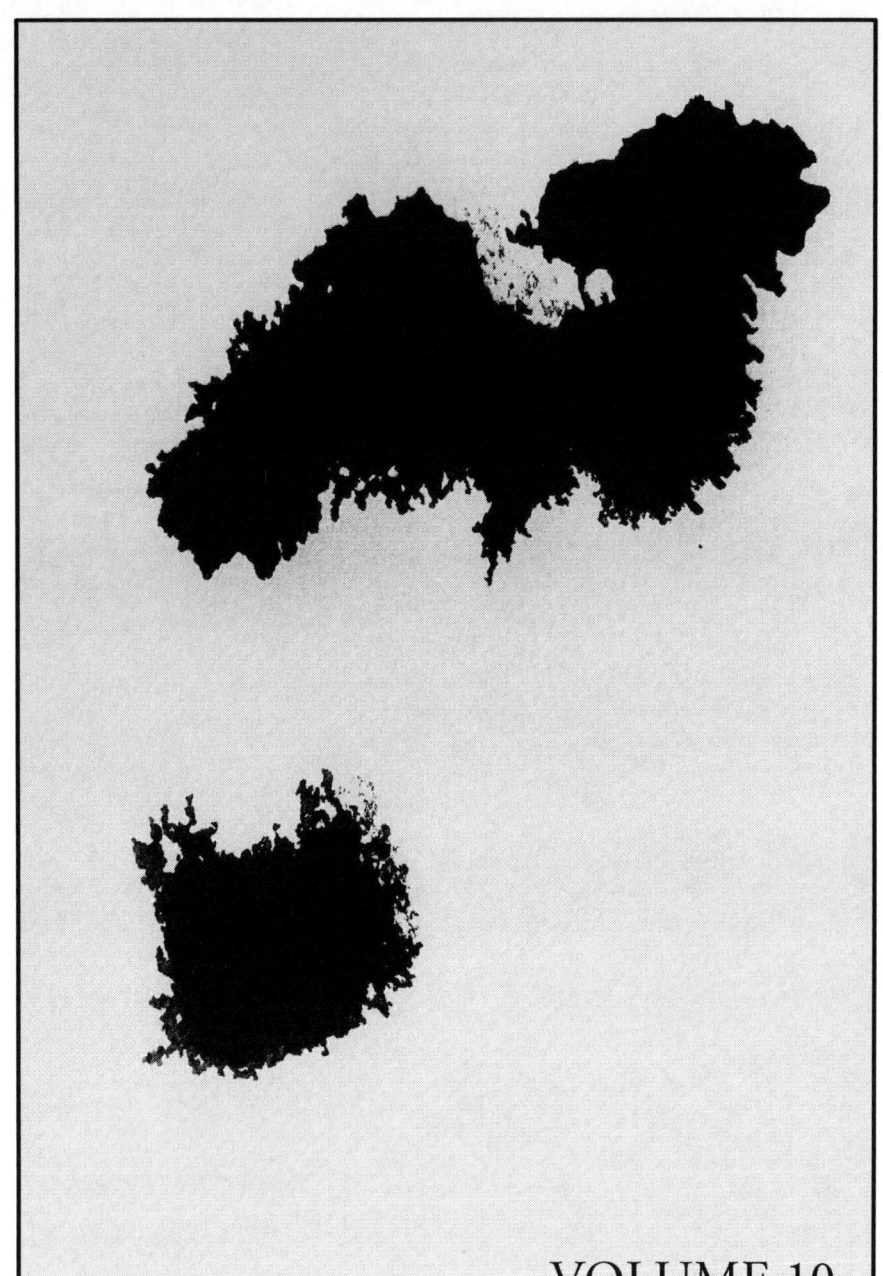

VOLUME 10.

Landing Party.

You have been placed ashore,
The Captain stands ankle deep in the water,
Never actually leaving the sea,
Landing craft beside her,
The ship is a mooring-rope length away.

Your eyesight has returned,
Slowly the final dressings are removed
The light, the colour, comes in again.

With unbandaged eyes, it is harder still to describe the ship.
A tree, a fish, perhaps a crab or turtle, threaded with fungi,
Coated with mosses and lichens, barnacles, seaweed.
The Captain never told you how she came to pilot it,
Where she found it,
What its history is.

The Captain unmasks too,
Unraveling the bandages from her head,
Allows you to see and look upon her face,
Just a young woman's face,
But under the skin,
Under the translucent covering of her eyes,
Beneath her lips,
Within the very structure of her hair,
Is everything of the ocean and nothing of the land.
She is the sea.

You ask why you are being put ashore,
And she tells you,

Now that you have listened to all her travels past,
And new shared travels with her,
That you can understand,
What's left of us,
It is being eroded.
It will crumble.

'We are off the map of the future,
that territory is lost.
I've not given you a world to claim.
Only the chance to marvel,
at its vastness.
These islands are a lullaby for our species'.

You ask the Captain where she is going.

'Into the weird waters,
and those who follow will share my future,
where everything that came before,
joins everything after.

There are islands that I have not taken you to,
An infinity emerging from waters,
They form at the horizon beyond our reach.

I cannot go there'.

VOLUME 10: ISLANDS.

Ark.

It is a small island notable for a large shipwreck on its rocky coast, and a population of all the wrong animals. At some point it is presumed that some individual or group built a real life Ark, with its guests collated from zoos, private collections or the wilderness. However the ship, while well built, had not been designed for seaworthiness, any glance would tell you it was unmaneuverable, lacking sails and engine, only a rudder. One expects they would sail with tides and steer around obstacles, or gently beach themselves on the shores of a future never to come. Instead it is presumed they crashed, early, against this former mountaintop. The ship remains in good condition, though it slowly rots, and will eventually fall apart.

The animals as such departed the hulk and found their way onto the shore, though this was not an accident. The wreckage reveals cages broken into for the outside, aquariums moved to the sea, tunnels cut into the hull to aid escape.

The animals have escaped from the rest of the world and found themselves in one place. A zoo-like concentration, excepting the lack of constraint.

The early days were not pleasant, nature in all its chaos, as various animals ate each other or lacking sufficient recognisable prey starved instead. Even the herbivores and omnivores poisoned themselves with inappropriate berries, roots and fruits.

But the island also provided – and animals that were strangers to each other more easily found relationships of symbiosis. Crows picking carrion from the open mouths of lions. Raccoons grooming the flies from the back of an elephant.

Animals much like each other interbred, and over time accidents became designs: Cogs, Egowls, Manapos.

What keeps people from the island is the abundance of wasps. Not your standard variety… large with long needles, not for predatory poison stings but for reproduction. The wasps are parasitic, and would normally plant their offspring in the bodies of grubs. But in the absence of their usual dance partners in this most apparently horrifying waltz of death and rebirth, the wasps have turned to planting their eggs in other species. The initial image of the wasp's offspring infesting and consuming rats and sparrows would be enough to damn the species as a monstrosity. Yet over time the hosts would begin to survive, adapting to this rough instruction, and like a gall their bodies would respond with pouches under the skin to accept the uninvited children. In turn something stranger and more wonderful began to occur, as each generation of rodent, mammal, and bird, adapted, so did the wasp. It picked up attributes from its host, soft fur or feathers, ears, an elongated tail. Not all the wasps as one new hybrid species, but a new invertebrate rainbow of variants emerging – each in turn seeking out the wrong animals to roll nature's dice with.

So many people will not approach the island, they consider it cursed, and monstrosity, but for others, it offers a hope. Is this not how the butterfly formed? Two species once distinct and averted, forced together by circumstance and in place of mutual extinction, merged and thrived. That which must die, might live through union with another.

Pools.

Ships must beware of these islands for they are numerous and near invisible, lying just beneath the surface at high tides and seas. Collections of them are worth charting on maps, to alert others to the risks, but also their rewards. They are made of the remnants of civilisation, old buildings and heaps of junk, but can also be natural formations of rock. As such they are still called rock pools. There are muscular starfish, sunrise-gold and pebble skinned, parading themselves across the aquatic sand on hundreds of delicate feet.

Despite being irregular in shape, made of barnacle edges, seaweed slopes, and slick black rock – each pool feels like a perfect circle. Despite each pool being full of seawater, sand, and the bodies live and dead of many forms of life and all their waste – each pool feels pure. They are still. The wind barely touches their surfaces due to the protection of the rocks, the tide cannot push or pull while out, and the life within is too small to trouble the water's surface for more than a moment or two. Only the occasional ripple from a fish, or tremor from a relocating crab disturbs the pools. Birds look, but rarely get the chance to swoop. Their pickings are reserved to what is caught out on the seaweed, and the already dead, with floating pale skin to the sun as the tide recedes.

The anemone, plump silk cushions frilled. In their grasp along with small organisms, are the grits of sand. The sand itself is a small polished world, and on them swarm bacteria, the grains of rock minerals and metals are landscapes, some grains of sand are plastic or bone that the bacteria are eating into, great lumps of the world. Like a piece of fruit the size of a continent had been placed on the horizon and all had swarmed to eat it.

For many in the world these are the watering holes and the oases of the seas, ships will carefully navigate to be near them and then collect small amounts of seaweed, crabs and fish before moving on. Ships anchoring here do so in an unwritten peace. There is no piracy here, Ships remain distant, only communicating over genuine needs: Fresh water, limited food, medical aid, navigational advice. Messages are often signaled, provisions left on outcrops, crews observing each other but rarely meeting. Even ships that know each other, restrain themselves from breaching this code of conduct here.

Too small and fragile to support our appetites, we have already learnt to preserve them, not to linger too long and despoil them, to leave as little of ourselves, our remaining culture among our reclaimed remnants.

Pebbles.

The island is a pebble Beach, soft slopes and banks like folds of cloth, but made of multitudes of rounded polished stones. Small rounded pebble, next to small rounded pebble. There is nothing else to it. A grey cloud resting in the ocean.

It is bookended on either end by two sets of boats anchored a few hundred feet away. Those who live on the boats are the custodians of the island. They live by fishing, farming seaweed, and gathering drinking water in large canopies. Occasionally a boat will depart for some period of time to work for another island nearby in exchange for goods and supplies. The work is seasonal and the islanders are valued due to an extremely strong work ethic and meticulous nature.

Before each dawn each day, they leave their boats and swim to the island. They never shore their boats. As the glow of the approaching sun reaches the island, they form a line side by side and slowly wade ashore. They carry only an empty bag slung over their shoulders. They face in the direction of the rising sun, but then turn their backs to it, look down, and judge the light by the clarity of the stones at their feet. If they can see the position of each stone clearly they can begin – and so, on some wordless signal of agreement they crouch, survey the stones, reach for the first that presents itself to them and move it from where it rests, into a new position.

The motion is calm, and swift, with only the briefest of pauses in the air, the stone suspended in their light touch like a chess piece mid-manoeuvre. The pebbles are sometimes turned and rotated, regarded to judge the best orientation. When placed they can be nestled into gaps, balanced on the edge of two adjacent stones, or rested atop a deeper laying pebble. No patterns are consciously made, no towers are built. Once a pebble is returned, one would not notice it had been moved.

Once the pebbles around them are placed to their liking, they take a single step back and repeat to the process. Throughout the day they work, with the sun arching over their curled backs to eventually tan their faces as it sets. They in turn retreat across the island leaving an invisible trail of rearranged pebbles in their wake. Eventually they step back into the sea, and as the tide begins to nudge the objects of their correction, they stop. They turn and submerge themselves, and swim to the boats anchored off the other side of the island.

Those that live and work here have a particular set of beliefs, that the world is broken and corrupted, but somewhere, perfection is just a small adjustment away – and if one were to correct it there among the pebbles, if a small area of the world were arranged perfectly, then the next move would be easy to see. Gleaming perfection would mark out squalid imperfection – and each correction to follow would suddenly be simple – like a jigsaw falling into place – and then onto and onto and onto the rest of the world exponentially increasing in speed and magnitude and subtlety, so that each part of the world could be made perfect, so that even a single perfect thought might not just arrive, but arrive perfectly formed, at the right time, expressed with elegance, ready for application, communication or contemplation.

Glass.

Once in a desert they built a city, made of glass, a corridor of splendour. Protected from and gleaming in the sun. Inside was luxury and perfection and peace. Water flowed, trees grew, birds sang and flew. People lived in clean, cool spaces. There were great bazaars that sold the very best of everything that could be gathered from the world, and every kind of entertainment and leisure.

The city was an act of defiance against the barren sand, against the punishing heat of the sun and against the changing world outside. They had no idea what was to come. It was also a perverse act of hope. Built sideways it did not dominate the sky, but rather sank into the sand, winding its way between the great dunes and vanishing in the rippling heat on the horizon. It showed the world that we had built could survive and adapt to the changes, survive oncoming inhospitability – to domesticate an expected catastrophe. This was what it was.

Now it is a wound erupting from the ocean and salt soaked sand. Various disasters befell it, there were fires, desertion, floods and riots. Soon the city was working against itself. Pipes bursting, wires sparking, structures collapsing. Then cracks began to appear at the edges of its great smooth exterior walls. These fault lines grew, following minuscule weakenings in the structure of the glass, like the cracks had minds of their own, seeking a shape or destination. If an outline were completed, tracing the coast of an unknown country, there would be a momentary pause, a minute, a day, a week, and then the colossal guillotine would fall.

Slate.

A smooth slab of dark stone, unevenly shaped, but flat, polished and near level with the horizon. The sea washes over it each night. The tide rises, and slow uneven lines of thin white foam ease over the surface, a gentle exploration to begin with. Silent, despite the sound of the ocean in the background. As the island is flat there is no retreat, each tidal advance keeps its ground it does not crawl back. The water spreads out and soaks into the pores of the rock, turning it from ash grey to black.

Soon the island is a convergence of curving lines making their way to the centre, as if there had several explosions around a central point and their shock waves rushing to meet. Weak pulses of tide leave lines further back, stronger pulses carry the ridges of foam forwards to make one dominant mountain range. Sometimes a small fragment of matter from the sea is tumbled up onto the tabletop. Some plastic wreckage, a strand of globular dark green weed, the floating body of a crab, upturned, the pale segments of its body drying in the sun in high contrast against the jet black frame. For a brief moment at the arrival of the tide each day, the island gleams, and creates a display of miniature artefacts, flotsam and jetsam.

If you stand on the island just at the moment when the sea is placing a skin of water on its top, the table turns to mirror, and the sky is reflected there and the objects are set in the blue above; As are you, you look down to see your reflection standing in the heavens. But then the waters push in circling waves in a single motion surging across the doubled vista, the foam crashes into the centre, then rolls back taking everything it offered cruelly back. Muddier, darker waters take their place and the sky vanishes from beneath you, and you are left standing studying the sea. The sensation is reversed, the tide does not rise, instead the island seems to sink away and you must swim. There is no island, the tides are unpredictable, and when it returns, it is new again.

Dream.

The Captain spoke, 'I have never seen this island, I have heard no rumour of it, but I have dreamt of it, and so I trust that it exists.

Boundless, unmeasured, unseen and untouched by humans, it is nothing but flowers.

They fan out leaves to catch the sun and rain, they grow petals, of every shape and design, simply because they can, simply for variations sake.

Every texture; blooms like silk, petals more thin and complex than a spider's web. Flowers more rugged and armour-edged than a crab's barnacle encrusted back.

Every colour in the spectrum, and those beyond all seeing eyes, fractal light explored, luminous. Gloss, matt, textured, smooth, angled curved, planes, pockets, paths, surfaces, patterns in every flower.

Imagine an orchid, unfolding to a rose, coarsening to a cactus, turning to lily, unravelling to fern, exploding into dandelion.

Stems and stalks, furred, or brittle, hard and tree like, woody, all upright or coiling, drooping under the weight, holding flowers aloft.

Procreation reinvented, genders multiplied, many and neither at once, self-replicating, spawning, pairing, coupling, interbreeding, splicing, parasitising, forming symbioses, duplicating.

At the shore of the island there are flowers known, the flowers known to every form of life. But other life is not permitted here.

The flowers pollinate themselves, germinate themselves, their roots churn the earth as worms would. Is it only flowers, and from that edge onwards, no other flower has a name.

They are infinitesimal and mountainous, unfettered by the restraints of gravity, or miniaturisation. Geography and Weather only seems to serve them.

In wind struck sections of the island great tangled threads of seeds are blooming on verdigris wings, emerald parachutes, and balloons of moss and lichen.

In the heat of the sun Cacti mass and squat bulbous in conference, or loom, fiercely spiked above.

Amid the rains, putrid flowers, offering lush temptations of scent and fruit, heavy-leaved and ropy-stalked, grow for the sake of excess.

In cold climes the smallest flowers find purchase to root on tips of frost.

It will never be discovered.

The island boundless will go on.

The world will end in flowers.'

Shells.

[handwritten margin notes: recruits readers in messes... by accumulation of terms collective into an atlas]

Many of us will remember the feeling of searching a beach in the hope of finding the perfect sea-shell.

Porcelain smooth, subtle dry colours that are intensified when dipped in the sea. Asymmetrical forms that somehow feel as if they begin a pattern that never resolves itself, spiralling into infinity.

Each shell found is almost what you want, near perfect, but with some residual flaw. A scratch, a chip, a hole, a barnacle encrusted, a life still residing inside.

As if hiding a secret grey fleshy muscle, or ruddy miniature armoured limbs retreat back inside to avoid your investigation.

This particular isle offers satisfaction to that urge, a seemingly endless opportunity to seek perfection, and to be made content with imperfection.

It rises gently above calm waters. The waves themselves neither froth nor crash, but gently lap the fractal edge.

[handwritten notes: for all its words and dreaming adventures, the world without itself withholds]

[handwritten: the littleness of promises disappointed but just a little ...]

[handwritten: each island is a foray into perception and sensation, each time driven back by the tidal frames]

[handwritten: at split: catalogue of enchantments, our fractured tango with melancholic elusiveness]

[handwritten: completionism moving into melancholic existentialism]

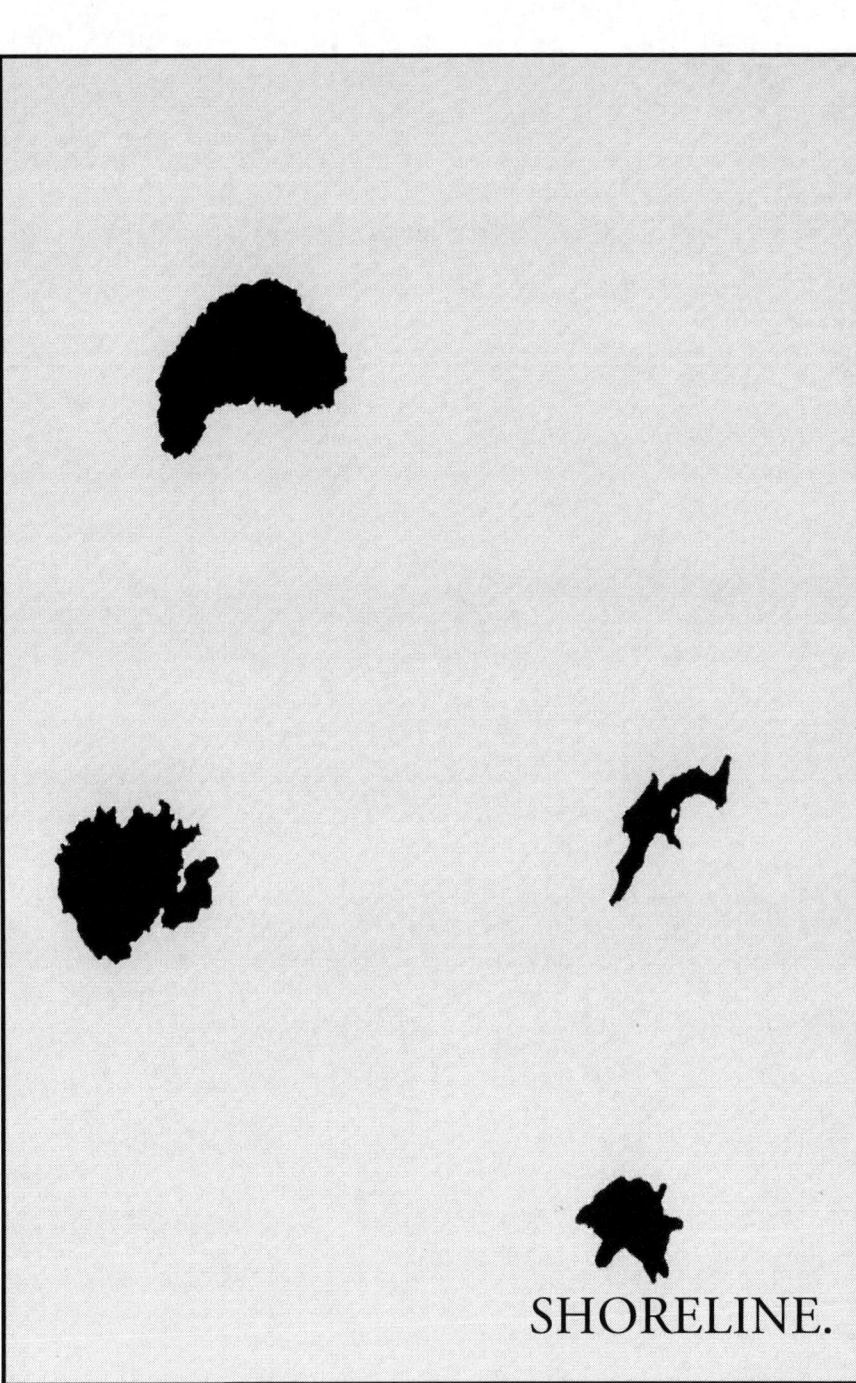

SHORELINE.

Shoreline.

You walk the beaches in your mind.
No Captain's voice, no hand at the rail.
Only the echo of her absence,
and the press of the islands against you.

You recite them as if they were prayers:
Cliffs, Mines, Buoys, Crocodiles, Flags, Pearl...
The names are ballast.
They keep you upright.

At first the atlas felt borrowed, fragile.

Now it feels heavier than your body.

You wonder if you are still remembering the islands, or if the
islands are remembering you.

The tide rises.
The tide falls.
You begin to speak aloud, though no one asks you to.

The shoreline calls,
And you cannot tell,
If it is the start of the sea,
Or the end of the land,
That you desire the most.

And here the wreckage of the world,
Is gathered up, and then ground down,
Till only a ribbon of time remains.

You can never be certain,
If it is the start of the land,
Or the end of the sea,
That you desire the most,
But the shoreline calls.

Go to the Cliffs,
Climb the Lighthouses,
Walk the Piers,
Raise high the Flags.
Descend the Mines,
Shape the Beaches,
Behold Crocodiles,
Circle the Buoys,
Stare into the Fire.

Gaze at Celestial bodies,
Touch the Summit,
Feel the hum of the Pylons,
Balance on Stilts,
Keep off the Grass,
Ring the Scaffolding,
Preserve the Monuments,
Tend the burnt earth,
Harness the Birds.

Run sticks along Fences,
Rummage in Plastic,
Walk the Walls,
Pick at the Dead,
Skate over Ice,
Ride to the Horizon,
Secure the Castle,

[handwritten marginalia:] fills up the space of fantasy with its props, a cluttered world of worlds, packed with "wonders" a "cradle" of bitterness...

[handwritten marginalia:] a feast for gluttonous tantrilits... how big a legacy childhood is...

[handwritten marginalia:] how the subjective stretches from unizon to horizon, populating the ones with its own archipelago

Dance upon Seashells,
Let the Fish take you.

Cling to the Rocks,
Dive Underwater,
Disarm every Weapon,
Ascend Skyscrapers,
Take the ropes of the Balloons,
Render the Fat,
Pick at the Bones,
Scream at the Themepark,
Let Leviathan sleep.

Wait out the Storm,
Cross the Bridges,
Wade through the Seaweed,
Dock at the Ports,
Leaf through the Paper,
Give witness to Ghosts,
Welcome the wasps,
Clamber up the Pebble Beach,
Mark the edge of the Void.

Dull the edge of the Glass and make it sing,
Make a Clean Slate,
Start your journey again.

Imagine the end.
Imagine the land disappearing,
Leaving only the ocean and the sky.
Then imagine the ocean and the sky recede,
Till only the void remains.
Then remember you will not be there to see the void.

AFTERWORD – LITTLE AHAB.

Afterword – Little Ahab.

You are now near the end of this book, and there is just a little left to go. Though the end can always be held off for a while, as you could write just a little more, you can pour more words in, and others too, just to hold off the end, for that little bit longer; we could invent new worlds, new life, new stories, we can hold off the end with invention; and isn't that what we've always done, starting a fire to hold off the night, telling stories, telling them again, and even if we don't exactly write new ones all the time we can just keep retelling and rearranging them, to breathe life into their embers again; and who would really know that the stories were circling, and rewriting themselves, and consuming and giving birth to themselves... to know that you would have to go back and read them again, and again, and remember them with such precision, that every word of every story was like a stone that you yourself had placed upon the ground to mark a secret place – only to find that on return, that others had done the same as you, and placed their stones, their words, their stories alongside yours.

-

A beach, many years ago near Saundersfoot, South Wales. I am rock-pooling with my brothers. They lead the way, I clamber afterwards with a bucket and spade. A gigantic Crab is what I'm searching for. I've seen a monstrous Man-Crab in my weekly horror comic, and I want to find that beast, or at least its living relative. Instead we find thick fleshed star-fish, anemone that grip our fingers, limpets and barnacles welded to the boulders. The cliffside shelters us from the sun as we search. Layers of rock. Millions of years, stacked up in order, then turned over, broken, and thrown about.

Then, there in a pool, a monster. Pale, and fleshy, floating, eyes up, tentacles adrift, frills resting. Dead. I know what it is, but I ask my brothers what it is regardless. A 'Cuttlefish', one says. In my mind, a submerged thought unlocks and is released. My search for the Crab has been abandoned, and I look out to sea. I am in my memory and imagination simultaneously, a mythic figure is becoming real. I've read of them in books, seen drawings, and watched them modelled in stop motion to monstrous effect in films. The science texts I read as a child said they existed, but no-one living had seen one, yet. I looked back at the cuttlefish, a proof of lineage, and I knew it must be real – The Giant Squid. Deep, pressured, cold, alive… As I looked back to the horizon, I thought 'If this dead thing is here, in a rockpool… then I know that it is out there, the Giant Squid, the Giant Squid, the Giant Squid'.

Acknowledgments:

This book is not mine alone. It carries the fingerprints of those who read it before it was ready, who questioned and encouraged me.

For every one of those early readers who offered their time, these islands are for you.

Very specific thanks to Adam at inkCONCRETE for cover design, setting the text, and literally publishing the book.

Thank you.